ANGEL HOUSE

(TY-ANGYLION)

MARK J.T. GRIFFIN

First Printed in 2011 in Great Britain
Copyright © 2011 by Mark J.T. Griffin

Cover Design

Mark J.T. Griffin

Published and Distributed by:

Power of One Ltd
Gryffyn House
Wyre Lane
Long Marston
Stratford upon Avon
CV37 6RQ

ISBN 978-0-9533017-6-8 (First Edition)

Website: www.markjtgriffin.com

Contents

For Ingrid, with All My Love

In Memory of
Piers and David
+
Bramble & Bracken

And the Angels

Acknowledgements

"A vision is the child of an idea. Ideas are the children of inspiration."

This book could not have been written without the help, encouragement and support of many and there are many without whom ideas could not have been transformed into print.

I would therefore like to acknowledge the following for their motivation, stimulation, inspiration, guidance, help or contribution to the development of this book:

Ingrid for her love, patience and encouragement

Dantje & Steph Jansen

For their Contribution:

Bill Mansell, Flo & Alan Talbot,

Piers Griffin, David Griffin, George & Millie Griffin,

Ethel, Flo, Clarrie & Hilda Williams, Ron & Dot Boxall,

Harold Reade, Molly Grupping-Dresens, Theo & Francina Grupping,

Theodora & Alfred Dresens

Bramble & Bracken

and

The Griffin and Grupping Families

Michael Moorcock, Douglas Adams,

Ridley Scott, Luc Besson, Robin Williams, Billy Connolly

Jack Black and Mindstore,

Rush, Marillion, Jon Anderson and Yes

Ann Roodt, Heather Wright, Jane Hamby

Bill & Gaynor Marshall

and

Sam and Lily for interrupting. A lot.

Author's Note

Those close to me will recognise many facets of the characters in "Angel House", not necessarily by name since names have been changed and the characters are often "conglomerates" – the inevitable writer's merging and remoulding of people, places and events - but certainly by the actions and/or words of the characters.

I realised in my early twenties the immeasurable input that my family have had in shaping and influencing my life.

As a young boy I was a bit of a loner, growing up in a huge family and finding solitude hiding under my bed with an old torch reading atlases and encyclopaedias. During the summer I spent six weeks with my grandparents in Dorset and sometimes spent Whit or Easter with my great-aunts in Wales.

Both sets of grandparents, great-uncles and great-aunts opened new experiences to me, in a small way such that my mind was open like a parachute to new thoughts. Music, art, literature were all introduced to me by the old and wise family rather than my parents. Perhaps that's why they are called "grand" or "great". I therefore thank them for giving me that initial peek into a bigger, wider, wonderful world. They have long since passed but I know they are still reading every word I write and occasionally guide me through life.

ANGEL HOUSE has been a joy to write and I hope that you find it as enjoyable to read as I found it to research and write.

Once again, many thanks to my friends, family and many others for their inspiration and encouragement to turn passing dreams into a reality; it would not have been possible without you.

May You Make Your Dreams Last Longer Than The Night...

September 2011

Prologue

Memories of Jason's earliest years to his teenage rebellion of 1976 are for the most part just camera flashes; incoherent snippets from a black-and-white movie in which one sees only a few disjointed frames. They are of climbing trees, playing on a home-made go-cart, rolling down grassy banks, swimming in the sea and his first kiss.

Most seem like a faded silent film and when they are viewed in the mind's eye he's struck by the lack of recognition he has for the boy. On the side table in his home in London he has a black-and-white photo of a giggling five-year old in shorts and t-shirt taken close up on a hot summer's day. Next to it there is a formal photo of the man in suit and tie. How the luggage, the daily burden of life, no more or less than any others, has taken its relentless toll on the lined face.

But memories of the summer of 1972 are as fresh and clear to him as if each moment was captured on celluloid or video, to replay over and over when the wish takes him.

His memories of those six weeks in 1972, which straddle his 3rd and 4th year at secondary school, are vivid and crystal clear. Every hour captured and filed, every moment savoured and enjoyed, even the ones that are perhaps tinged with a touch of sadness.

When one looks back to the summers of our youth we tend to view them with fondness. They were warmer, sunnier, freer, happier, longer and for Jason those summers were no different. All those superlatives are applicable. Jason cannot think of that summer without a smirk, a smile of thanks, for like a weedy sapling he began to grow sturdier and stronger from the experiences of those days.

Before he was just another spotty 13-year old in his own world of comics, mates, mucking around and football. Named after his mother's favourite film "Jason and the Argonauts", after his journey that summer he was more introspective, more understanding and yes, perhaps even wiser.

Sometimes, when questioned, he is asked why "he is as he is" and with gratification he can pinpoint the change of direction; the departure from childhood and beginning of the movement into youth towards maturity and adulthood to that summer.

For those that nurtured that growth Jason is deeply in debt; for they have long since passed, but their actions, words and ideas, the essence of their soul and spirit survives in these words, and in Jason's actions as an adult towards others. Their faces, voices, laughter and energy are as much a part of him as spirit, soul, flesh and bone. Not a day goes by when a lesson from those days is not replayed, not a moment when he is not thankful for the gift of the short days he spent in that home by the sea which before was a just house and afterwards a sacred space of love and joy.

But, to paraphrase the bard "we run before our time!"

We must start at the beginning.

1. The Heart of the Storm

"The difference between a person and an angel is easy.
Most of an angel is in the inside
and most of a person is on the outside."

Jason sat on the top step of the staircase and clutching the handrail, listened to the flaming row that raged in the lounge; his mother and father were at each other's throats again. Voices raised, things thrown and smashed, screams, sometimes slaps and shouts.

Jason had watched and listened frequently as he got older, even now he was only thirteen but as the years had drawn on the arguments had become more intense, his father grown angrier and his mother more sad.

Even to Jason, a mere boy, it seemed that they should throw in the towel and call it a day but in quiet desperation they hung on to their marriage. Perhaps it was for him, the only child, perhaps for social convention, perhaps for the house, the family. He didn't know. He did know that it was, and had been, having an effect on him.

It would always begin with a slammed door or a raised voice. An argument over a cold dinner or a bill or an untidy room or hot tea or whatever took their fancy at the time. It made no odds to Jason but in the semi-detached house that was his home, the walls, floors and doors were paper-thin. So thin that the neighbours could not have failed to know that Jason's parents' marriage was in trouble.

The door opened and he let go of the handrail and leaned back so he could not be seen. He saw his father's balding head dart towards the kitchen followed closely by his mother.

"Don't walk away from me! Don't you dare turn your back on me," she screamed.

"I'll do what I damned well please, whenever I want!" he shouted back.

Had these mature adults once loved each other? Had these humans held each other and kissed as lovers? Had they cried and laughed over the same sorrows and joys? If they had they had forgotten it now.

The kitchen door was slammed and the raging storm continued behind the door. Jason sighed and slunk back up the stairs and back to his bedroom.

He wasn't tired and could not sleep so he grabbed his atlas and torch and crawled under the bed. Pulling the candlewick down creating a tent he somehow felt more safe and secure beneath the bed rather than in it.

He leaned the atlas up against the legs of the bed and opened it at random. Europe. France, Germany, Austria, Belgium, Luxembourg, The Netherlands. He scanned the towns and cities as he had done many times before. He longed to visit each one but had absolutely no idea how he was ever going to escape and do it.

The possibility of travel – even into his hometown – was beyond his imagination. Sometimes he would recognise a town or city from reading or seeing pictures in the Sunday magazines, battered old copies of the National Geographic or travel brochures which his aunt brought him to flick through and he would dream of standing in the square or being on a boat on the river or canal.

He heard another bang and crash from below him. It was becoming more intense. He could hear muffled words and the usual range of insults thrown at one another with abandon in an attempt to hit some emotional target.

Jason's eyes were becoming tired and his torch dimmed suddenly. He hit the bottom of the torch in the vain hope that the batteries would yield more power but they stubbornly disobeyed. He switched it off and in the dim light closed the atlas and crawled from under the bed. He placed the atlas back in his library and pulling back the covers got into bed.

He could hear more muffled voices and shouts and he pulled the covers over his head to shut out the light and the rest of the world and closed his eyes.

Jason had been asleep for about an hour when his senses woke him by the door opening a few inches. He stayed under the covers and pretended to be asleep.

"So, you agree he should stay at my aunts? While we sort all this out," his father said.

"Yes; okay, it would at least give us a break over the summer, a breather. And him too. It can't be easy for him either," his mother replied.

Jason's father harrumphed and his mother whispered, "Night, night, Jason. We love you," and gently closed the door.

Jason lay for a moment, pulled back the bedclothes and breathed the fresh air again. "What was that all about?" he thought, "Well, I'll find out soon enough. Better get some sleep – school tomorrow."

Next morning Jason scurried around trying to find socks, shirt, tie, blazer, and all the usual school paraphernalia that incongruously seemed to grow legs and walk during the night.

"Mum! I've lost my tie!" he would shout to his mother.

"No Jason you haven't. It's not lost. You've just not looked in the right place," she would always reply rather unhelpfully.

Of course she was always right. He'd taken it off and put it in a blazer pocket or in his satchel or in the cloakroom. Never where it should be of course.

He hadn't really thought of the previous night – he tended to bury memories of a parental shouting match – when his mother said, "Jason, your Dad and I have had a great idea. We know how you loathe going on holiday with us to Scotland – we thought you'd like to go to the seaside for the whole summer. You'd enjoy that wouldn't you?"

"Well, I don't know, where do you mean?" Jason asked racking his brains as to where this could be.

"Well you know your father's aunts live in Aberdovey – on the Welsh coast – it's lovely up there and they've said they'd love to have you. You'd go by train and we'd give you some pocket money. You'll love it," she replied, selling the idea as if she was on commission.

"You mean Dad's aged aunts and the dotty uncle? You're joking! Mum! Please?" Jason said pleading but it was obvious that it was a done deal already.

His father walked in the kitchen and sat down before a bowl of cornflakes pre-poured by his wife. "So, what do you think? Six weeks by the sea – it will be great!"

"With a bunch of oldies? Then why don't you go!" Jason said, realising too late that this was crossing the line of respect, and his father immediately raised his voice in combat.

"Don't you dare answer me back! The impertinence! You ungrateful little…, If I had had the chances you've had…" and rising from the table he picked up his briefcase and walked out of the house, petulantly slamming the door behind him.

"See what you've done," his mother said and she tutted, "Well the arrangements are almost made. A week on Saturday we'll put you on the train." She dried her hands on the tea towel. "Now finish you breakfast."

And that was the end of it. Jason's summer was arranged. Another full week at school and he'd be away.

At first he was angry, then he sulked, then resigned himself to it. He always said he wanted to travel, go places. He should always be careful of what he wished for. He looked up the place in his atlas and traced the railway line from Wolverhampton where he lived to the Welsh coast and Aberdovey.

Last time he'd been there he'd been about five. He could remember a picnic with all the family, including his great-grandfather and grandfather and all these other relatives in this park across from the house. He could only really remember the sandwiches. They'd been salmon and cucumber, with the crusts cut off.

Well six weeks wasn't that long. He'd take his atlas and a few comics and he'd be fine. Six weeks would go very quickly.

That night he cried. He didn't know why, he just felt like he wasn't in control of his circumstances. He'd had no choice in the matter. It wasn't that he didn't want to go, it was just that he'd have liked to have been asked. He cried himself to sleep; it wasn't the first time and it wouldn't be the last. For as much joy in the world there is as much sorrow. He learned that very early in his life but hadn't yet realised it.

Later in the week Jason, homework done, was about to slip into bed when he heard the phone ring. His father answered it in his usual gruff and business-like way. Jason opened his bedroom door so he could at least hear one half of the conversation.

"Ah, hello Aunt Maud. Yes we are both well."

"Yes. We plan to put Jason on the early train so he arrives just after lunch."

"No, it's a through train. He won't have to change. Let me see… it arrives at Penhelig at 1:35."

"And you'll meet him. Good."

"Yes, I'll make sure Irene will pack all those things for him. Yes."

"Oooh. In the attic? Yes, he should be no trouble to you up there."

"No I think that's about it. Oh wait. How will you send us the cost of the train fare?"

"Well I thought you would pay as you said you'd give him a holiday."

"Well even the child fare, he's 13 but looks 11, is £3.70 and we'll have to give him some pocket money of course."

It was clear Aunt Maud was taking no nonsense. "There's no need to take that tone Aunt. If you're going to be like that we'll not send him at all!" his father said, almost raising his voice.

"Okay. That seems fair. Then we will have to agree to disagree. Yes, I'll pay half." Then with a thought he added, "You pay for the ticket which we can pick up at the station and I'll send you a cheque."

"Yes. Okay. We'll call to confirm he's on the train in the morning."

"Yes. Best wishes to my aunts and Uncle Jack. Yes, goodbye."

Jason always cringed when his father quibbled over money, trying to get his aunts to pay the train fare. Whenever Jason had to ask for 50p for a school trip he'd always get the "third degree". Where was he going? Why was he going? Could he not go?

He closed the door and took an old photo album from his library on the floor and sat on the bed. He flicked the pages and opened it to two pages of photos taken on the picnic in Aberdovey when he was around five years old.

The photos were in black and white and quite small but he was sitting on the grass with a ball in front of five aged women and two old men.

He unclipped the photo from its black mounts and examined it further. He didn't recognise the people in the photo except himself of course. He turned it over. The tiny writing by his mother on the back of the photo said:

"Jason, Agnes, Hettie, Emily, Grandpa Hughes, Jack and Clarissa. Penhelig Gardens. July 1964."

He took his magnifying glass and holding the photo in his thumb and forefinger examined it like a detective under the light of the bedside lamp.

They all looked so old, all lavender and liniment, walking sticks and wheel chairs, even eight years ago. He sighed. What would he do for six weeks in the summer with a bunch of pensioners? They were bound to get him to help and do chores and read books and just talk and talk and talk.

He slammed the album shut with the picture tucked inside the front cover and went to clean his teeth. As he did so his mother called up the stairs:

"Jason! Are you in bed yet?"

Jason mumbled a shout of "Yesh! Ssschoon!" through a mouthful of toothpaste which he spat out with venom.

Tomorrow was the last day before school broke up for the summer. He didn't have many friends but those he did have were all going to Spain or France or even one to Australia to visit relatives. Why didn't he have relatives in Australia?

He tutted at his family's misfortune and climbed wearily into bed. It was only just dark and though his body was ready to lie down his brain was still turning over the events of the day.

Half an hour later he closed his eyes and drifted into a deep and relaxing sleep.

He dreamt only one dream that night before his journey. It was a dream that at the time he could not comprehend. It was strange and mystical, ethereal and of a heavenly quality.

It was of a beautiful smiling girl with long blonde tresses dressed in a flowing calico-white cotton dress. She laughed with joy and glee and lifted glowing balls of fire that floated into a starlit indigo night sky.

2. Over the Border

"We are each other's angel.
We meet when it is time."

On the Friday evening Jason and his Mum packed an old leather suitcase with two changes of clothing, and a leather-look shopping bag – handles worn with overuse – with a few comics, his atlas and a packed lunch for the journey.

She winked at him, "I've put in a chocolate bar for you but don't tell you Dad." Then she took her purse and took out a pound note. "Don't tell your Dad about this either," she said.

She kissed his forehead and Jason smiled like a cat that'd got the cream. He folded the note up small and tucked it safely in his trouser pocket. He was ready to go.

That night he didn't sleep well and was filled with a combination of excitement and apprehension.

The next morning, after a good breakfast, Jason's father put the suitcase and bag into the boot of their Austin 1300 and drove to the station.

They stopped outside. "Irene, Aunt Hettie said there would be a ticket waiting for you - if you pick it up and put Jason on the right platform I'm going to drive round the block until you get back. Be as quick as you can."

"Are you not going to give Jason a bit of pocket money?" his mother asked.

"No! Whatever for?" his father said, dismissing the very idea and he shrugged, "My aunts will see him right. Come on, hurry up I can't wait here or I'll get a ticket."

Jason was ushered out of the car. Flustered his mother opened the boot and took out the suitcase and bag, and with a perfunctory wave his father turned the car around and drove back the way he came.

His mother went to the ticket booth to collect Jason's ticket. "I've got a ticket reserved – a single - child to Aberdovey in the name of Hughes."

"Certainly madam. It's paid for but there's a surcharge for the post of 10 pence," the clerk answered politely. His mother tutted and pushed a coin over the counter.

"And what platform's it on?" she asked.

"Platform 1," said the man looking at the clock, "leaving in five minutes, just through the gates there."

Jason's mother took him to the gate and then crouched down and kissed his cheek. "Now you be good and don't get on your aunts' nerves. Will you write to me too – at least once a week?" Jason nodded.

Then his mother kissed him again and said something she had never said to him before. "I love you Jason. I love you very much."

Jason was a little embarrassed but replied, "I love you too Mum. I'll miss you."

His mother nodded and Jason could see the tears welling up in her eyes.

Then she heard a car horn and turned to see her husband pulling up outside the station again.

"I'd better go," she said and placing a hand on his back pushed him through the gate. "You be good now," and with a wave she ran back to the car.

The porter looked down at Jason from under his peaked cap.

"Off on your holidays son?"

"Aberdovey. Six weeks," he replied and held back a tear.

"Oh you'll love it! It not far and there's ice cream and sand and all sorts. Me and the missus have day trips up there sometimes. We get it cheap of course, being on the railway."

17

Then he looked down the track and could see an engine pulling its load towards the platform.

"Now, you wait by that bench there," the porter said and he tapped his nose, "and I'll find you a good seat."

The blaring Tannoy announced the train's arrival: "The train now approaching Platform 1 is the 08:35 Welsh Coast Line Train from Birmingham New Street to Pwllheli calling at Shifnal, Oakengates, Wellington, Shrewsbury, Welshpool, Newtown, caarrrrssss... bluurrrdeblurr... gargar... passengers.... blarrr blarrr...front of the train for all stations from... blargar...." The rest was drowned out by the roar of the diesel engine pulling eight carriages thundering into the station. For a moment Jason could do little but step back feeling, inexplicably, that the beast would suck him under its iron wheels onto the track.

There was a bit of commotion then the porter came over to him.

"Right! Second Class seat for you close to the front of the train. Safer to put you in an open compartment and I'll get the guard to keep an eye on you," he said opening the door.

"There you go. You have a great time. Find yourself a seat by the window. You'll get a great view as you go along the coast."

Jason shuffled along the aisle and found a seat of four with a table to himself. He put his suitcase under the seat and placed the shopping bag beside him. Very few people got into the carriage with him and it was quiet on the train. A few moments later the train lurched and began its journey to the west and the Welsh marshes.

Jason sat back and enjoyed the view, such that it was, through the industrial estates and past the factories of the West Midlands. It was an inspiring sight but soon it was behind them and the train sped out of the West Midlands and towards Shropshire.

He remembered a story he'd been told about how on her journey to Scotland and her home at Balmoral Queen Victoria had asked what the tunnel was her train was going through, as it seemed to be very long. This, she was told, was not a tunnel but the Black Country. Henceforth the blinds of the train were closed at Coventry and opened again at Stafford.

After an hour or so the train began to labour up towards the Welsh border at Newtown and pulled in at Welshpool. Jason, who could smell the bacon sandwiches from the buffet at the station, now became peckish and even though it was very early he decided he'd have an early lunch, and he emptied the shopping bag on the plastic-topped table before him.

It contained a greaseproof paper bag of cheese and Branston-pickle sandwiches, a bag of plain crisps with a little bag of salt, a Mars bar and a carton of Kia-ora orange juice that always tasted like plastic as far as Jason was concerned.

He also took out the two comics he had brought with him, The Dandy and The Beano, and placed them in front of him. Truth be told he was probably too old for them now but they were old copies and he liked to see how the characters had been drawn.

Strangely enough they bored him very quickly and he again began to admire the view, the sheep on the hills, bramble, hedgerows, cuttings and embankments and at some point they crossed the border into Wales.

Before too long he'd finished his packed lunch (having splodged pickle down his shirt as he always did) and had packed the rubbish tightly into the bins. The train was pulling into the sleepy market town of Machynlleth, ancient seat of the Welsh William Wallace, the revolutionary Owen Glyndwr.

As the train pulled away once more the guard checked his ticket again. "Now you're getting out next but one stop. So we stop at Dovey Junction, then it's your stop at Penhelig. If you get to Aberdovey you've gone too far!"

The train left Machynlleth and wound its way slowly along the Dovey estuary until it widened and they stopped in what appeared to be the middle of a muddy riverbed at Dovey Junction. One way headed south to Aberystwyth, the other north towards the coastal towns of Aberdovey, Barmouth, Porthmadog and Pwllheli and all stations in between.

They decoupled the four carriages at the rear of the train that were to go to Aberystwyth and again the train lumbered forwards hugging the north coast of the estuary which gradually opened out into tidal waters.

By now the carriage had emptied so Jason got up, opened the window and gingerly stuck out his head. On the far side of the estuary he could see the caravan sites of Borth, Ynslas Sands, to his right the open sea and occasionally a glimpse of the harbour at the estuary mouth of Aberdovey.

He returned to his seat and made sure he had all his things ready. The train went through a short tunnel and came to a noisy and slow grinding halt at Penhelig.

The raised wooden platform, built on a bridge and made from railway sleepers, was empty and at first he didn't know whether he should get out. Then the guard appeared.

"Come on sonny! Off you get! This is your stop," he cried from the back of the train.

Jason put his suitcase on the platform and hopped down and with a shout and a whistle the train pulled away again, leaving him alone on the quiet, empty platform. He looked around and thought he'd better sit on a bench and wait.

A few minutes later an old lady walked quickly along the platform towards him.

"Jason! Jason Hughes. That is you isn't it?" she called. "Come on Jason. It's me. Your Aunt Hettie!"

She was in her late seventies and wore a blue cotton dress and carried a blue leather handbag. She also wore a blue felt hat with a peacock brooch pinned to it. Her smile was warm and inviting but her demeanour was busy and no-nonsense.

Jason picked up his bag and they walked to the steps that took them down to road level.

His aunt verbally machine-gunned him with a barrage of questions, which Jason felt were probably rhetorical anyway.

"Did you have a good journey? Of course you did. What's that down your front? Pickle? Tut. Well it will wash out I'm sure. Do you need the toilet? Well come on, it's not far. Can you manage your suitcase? It's not much for six weeks is it? Here let me take your shopping bag."

Then they walked under the bridge where cars passed a few inches from where they walked and they clung as close to the wall as they could.

"Be careful, there's no pavement here," she said and to Jason's surprise they climbed the stone steps at the house right next to the bridge.

Jason grasped the iron hand rail, put his foot on the bottom step and looked up at the imposing three-storey house.

His aunt turned and looked down the steps to where her nephew had stopped. "It's called Ty Angylion, she said."

The early afternoon sun glinted off the windows then his aunt added "It's Welsh for The House of Angels. We sometimes call it 'Angel House'."

3. House of Angels

Angels Around You
Finding a Tiny White Feather
A Sudden Sweet Fragrance Under Your Nose
A Bright Light or Colour in the Mind's eye
Tingling in the Air
A Feeling of Loving Warmth

Aunt Hettie unlocked the front door and they stepped inside. She took off her coat and hung it on the wooden lattice coat stand on the wall and then unbuttoned her grey cardigan.

"Welcome to Ty Angylion," she said in perfect Welsh, "now, hang up your coat, leave your case there and we'll sort you out. Would you like water, tea or orange squash?"

"Do you have lemonade?" Jason asked.

"Lemonade! Goodness no! What use have we got for lemonade? No, it's water, tea or squash or nothing at all."

"Squash then," Jason said slightly crestfallen.

"Squash then what?" his aunt asked searching for the magic word.

"Sorry. Yes. Squash, please aunt," Jason said apologetically.

"That's better, now take a seat in the front room and I'll put the kettle on and see if I can find the others."

She disappeared into the back kitchen tapping the barometer in the hall and as she did so added "Fine. Mmm. Good!"

Jason walked into the front room. A huge bay window overlooked the small park gardens across the road from the house and the estuary and the hills beyond.

It had a window seat constructed in it so that one could sit and with one eye enjoy the view and the cars go by the window, and at the same time read with the other.

The room itself was not large but had a sofa and easy chair facing the fireplace. Jason scanned the room for a television but could see none. Perhaps in the other room, he surmised.

On the opposite wall from the window was a glass-fronted cabinet full of ornaments and pictures and vases.

Jason heard a cry from the hall as Aunt Hettie called up the stairs.

"Girls? Jack?" she called, "Are you about?"

Jason heard a couple of "Comings" and "Woo-hoos" in reply and then footsteps crossed the creaky floor upstairs and came down the carpeted stairs.

A face appeared round the door and entered the room. It was an old lady, her grey hair still with some flecks of black in it.

She smiled and crossed the room and kissed his cheek. "You must be Jason. I'm your Aunt Agnes."

Jason looked into Agnes's cornflower-blue eyes and realised that she would have been a very beautiful woman once but the ripples of time had left their mark. She was in her mid-seventies and wore a green print dress with a belt at the waist. She wore brown brogue lace-up shoes. On her left hand she wore a wedding ring but Jason had not realised she had been married.

Hettie entered the room and handed Jason a plate with a biscuit on it and a glass of orange squash. This flummoxed Jason at first, as he could sip the squash but couldn't eat the biscuit without putting down the plate. In the end he balanced the plate on his lap.

Jason looked up at Hettie and smiled weakly; he realised she still had her hat on, which apparently was her normal practise, to wear her hat in the house.

Hettie darted him a look and he came out of his day dream. "Now don't you dare spill it on my cushions," and then turning to Agnes who had taken a seat on the sofa added, "where are the others?"

Agnes shrugged. "Emily and Maud are on their way down and Jack's having his nap. I think Clarrie popped into town for some milk and bread – we were running a bit low."

"Bit low?" Hettie said, "We have plenty. Gosh my little sister can be silly sometimes. Easy plenty. What a waste," she added sternly.

"Just coming!" There was another call from upstairs and moments later another face appeared at the door.

"Jason! How wonderful to see you. We were just getting your room ready. You're way up in the stars almost!" It was his Aunt Maud and she kissed his cheek and squeezed his hand. "Gosh you're much bigger than I remember you – you must have been four, five maybe."

"I was five, I think," Jason said nervously.

Maud was in her early seventies and very thin; she wore a black skirt with a twin set and string of pearls; she wore horn-rimmed thick glasses and little jewellery except for a gold watch on her wrist, which she kept fiddling with.

"Just so, five, we had a picnic over the road in the gardens. A beautiful day as I remember," Hettie added. "You were very good for five. Quiet and well behaved and I hope that has not changed. We stand no nonsense here do we?" and she turned to her sisters for agreement but they just smiled not wishing to agree or disagree.

"Emily was on her way down but she takes the stairs a bit easier these days. She's the eldest you know," Maud added.

Jason nodded and thought "The eldest. They all look 'eldest'," but said nothing.

Emily came through the door. She also wore thick spectacles and walked with a stick and was shown to the easy chair. She wore a blue and white cotton print dress with black shoes and had a slight limp.

"Come over and say hello to your Aunt Emily then?" Hettie prompted and Jason carefully put plate and glass on the marble hearth and kissed Emily on the cheek.

"Sorry I couldn't come over," Emily said, "my legs are okay but I can't see as well and I tend to trip over things."

As Jason kissed Emily on the cheek Aunt Clarissa entered the room.

"Hello all!" she said and then went over to Jason and kissed his cheek, "You won't remember me, only a babe when I last saw you." Then she looked around and smiled, "So what are we doing? Do we have tea and cakes? Good, of course we do? Yum!"

24

Clarrie was younger than the rest and she was the sort of person that lit up a room. Her energy seemed boundless but she was very scatty and her mind seemed to flit from subject to subject like a butterfly.

She was quite tall and not as skinny as Maud or Hettie but by no means fat; she wore a white drop-waisted skirt and a scarf around her neck in rather a Bohemian fashion.

"Are we all here? I could eat a horse!" she said to no one in particular.

"I think we're almost all here so I'll go and fetch the tray." Hettie went off to the kitchen and returned with the tea tray and cups and saucers and more biscuits.

"Pull that table over here," she said to Jason. "That's it in front of the sofa," and as he did so she bent and carefully put the tray on it. She sat down on the sofa and Maud sat opposite Jason in the window seat while tea was poured.

Maud gazed off into the distance across the estuary and over towards Borth and Ynslas. "It's a bonny day girls. I was in the back garden earlier – it's chilly but warming up nicely," she said.

"Are you looking forward to your holiday Jason?" Emily asked.

"Yes," Jason said nervously.

"What do you want to do?" Agnes asked.

"Well I'm not sure," Jason replied. "I'm not sure what you can do here."

"Not sure?" Hettie replied quickly, "Lots! Walks, fresh air, we've got books, games, all sorts. You can help around the house. We'll keep you busy, don't you worry young man."

Jason didn't like the sound of that. Not one little bit.

"Now don't be hard on the lad Hettie," Emily said disapprovingly, "the boy's on his summer holiday after all."

"Well I'm not having any lazing around. Idle hands make…" Hettie said but was cut short by Maud "…make a dull boy?" she added and Agnes chuckled while Hettie tutted at their impertinence.

"Now Jason? Do you remember us all? Do you know who we are?"

At first Jason said nothing and stared nervously not wishing to make a slip and get things wrong and he realised that Hettie's sternness was making his shyness worse. Finally after a few 'umms' and 'aahhs' he pointed towards his Aunt Maud and said, "I think I remember you, Aunt Maud, and you, Aunt Agnes, but I don't remember you or Clarissa," he said directing his comment to Hettie who shrugged.

"It's Aunt Clarrisa," Hettie said correcting him, "and I think she was off on one of her walks most of the day. I don't remember playing with you too much – I was far too busy."

"I know!" Agnes said, "It must be bewildering for the poor lad," and Jason smiled politely. "Why don't we show him on the family tree?"

"Good idea!" Maud replied and left the room returning a few moments later with a folder.

"Agnes's been working on this for years, it's very rough of course and nowhere near complete but the chart will help," Maud said opening a lever arch file and turning to a chart, which she folded, open. She shuffled along the window seat and Agnes sat down beside her.

"Now this here is you – born 1958 to Irene and Jason Hughes. Jason, like you, was an only child and Jason's father was Charles Hughes," Maud said.

"Now Charles was the oldest boy of a huge family, most of whom you see around you," Agnes continued, "After Charles, who died nearly seven years ago in 1966."

"The day after England won the world cup," Clarrie said helpfully, then added, "England 4 - West Germany 2. Geoff Hurst hat-trick and Martin Peters."

"Yes; then in order there was Emily born in 1891 which makes her 81, I was born in 1893 which makes me 79, Hettie born in 1901 which makes her 71, then Maud born in 1896 which makes her 76, then the babies Jack born in 1898 which makes him 74 and.."

"And I'm the baby. Born 1912 and a slip of a girl at 60!" Clarrie piped up and she fluttered her eyelashes alluringly, much to Maud's disgust.

"Such nonsense," Maud said under her breath then added whilst shaking her head at Clarrie's frivolity, "so there you have it Jason."

And she folded back the family tree, "The only one you haven't met is your Uncle John. Never been called John of course, always Jack since he was a boy."

"Jack the lad we called him!" Clarrie butted in again, "Wait, I'll call him again," and before she could be stopped she was at the bottom of the stairs.

"No, don't Clarrie. He could be taking his nap!"

But it was too late and Clarrie called in a shrill voice, "Jack! Jack! Come and meet your grand-nephew!"

Again a muffled "Coming" was heard in reply and then Jason heard footfalls on the steep stairs. A few moments later a head peaked from around the door.

It was Jack, his eyes were bright blue buttons which twinkled with life and excitement.

"Ah, Jason my lad!" and Jack put out a hand in greeting to Jason who stood up and shook it.

"Most polite my boy. Well done! Manners maketh you know!" Jack said with a flourish.

Jack was dressed in a tweed jacket and a pair of grey trousers and brown brogue shoes; his checked shirt had a light-brown pattern and was slightly creased.

"Been taking my afternoon siesta; good for the body and soul, don't you know," he said, "usually finished up with a cuppa and a biscuit to accompany me tea!" and smiling at Hettie she took the hint and poured him the last of the pot.

She handed him the china cup nestled on a patterned saucer and placed a shortbread biscuit on it.

"Ah, something to dunk," he said, dunked the biscuit, took a bite and took a sip of tea. He swallowed and made a loud "ahhhh!" sound to show his total satisfaction at the combination.

"So, what are your plans young Jason?" but before he had a chance to answer Jack asked "And do you like Shakespeare?"

"He's a boy of 13!" Hettie said, "Haven't met a 13-year old who ever did!"

Jason stuttered, still taken aback by the question, "Well we did some at school – 'Romeo and Juliet' but it was very…," and he struggled for a word, "…boring."

"Yes. Would be. Needs to be performed yer see! Rome and Jules is pretty dire for a boy. All the romantic sissy stuff. You want a good tragedy like 'Hamlet' or 'King Lear' or a history Rick 3 or 'Henry Fifth'" and Jack launched into: "Oh for a muse of fire…".

Maud realised Jack was onto his pet subject, "Jack will you do us a big favour and top up the pot for us? And perhaps more biscuits too!"

Before Jack managed to get to the next line he had been cut short and with an "Of course, of course" was ushered into the kitchen.

Hettie took control "Well Jason, we must show you your bedroom. It's on the top floor, a good climb but a wonderful view over the estuary. You can see Ynslas Sands and people driving on the beach quite clearly on a sunny day. Now Clarrie, while Jack's making a fresh brew why don't you take Jason up to his bedroom."

Clarrie clapped her hands. "Wonderful idea!" she said excitedly. "We might see a train from the landing window too!"

"A train?" asked Jason.

"Oh, yes, the run from Machynlleth up the coast to Pwllheli on the hour. You can set your watch by them."

"Don't have a watch," Jason said

"No watch?" Clarrie said, "Well we must sort that out as soon as possible! Come on! Up the wooden bank!"

And grabbing his case Jason followed Clarrie as they climbed the stairs. Its steepness was such that it was absolutely essential to hold on to the polished oak handrail.

On the first landing Clarrie took a breath, turned and pointed to the window. "Trains. On the hour. Got to be quick though. Sometimes they toot." Jason glanced and could see the railway tunnel behind the house.

On the landing there were four doors leading to three bedrooms and a bathroom.

"Maud, Emily, Hettie," she pointed. "Now. Next floor! Come on!" and they continued the climb.

On the next landing there were another four doors.

"Jack, bathroom, Agnes and me!" there was a painted white-enamel plaque on the door which said 'Clarrie' with a picture of a sunflower.

Jason sniffed the air and realised that the pervading smell on both of the upper floors was of rose, lavender and eau de cologne.

"One more!" said Clarrie and they climbed a short flight to a small landing with two doors. "WC with a sink to the left AND...." she said with a flourish throwing the door open "...your residence for the next few weeks."

The room was spacious with a brass bed and lumpy mattress covered with a pink candlewick bedspread, a dark-oak wardrobe, dressing table and a good-sized window, which, as promised, looked out on the front of the house and over the estuary.

"Now I'll just nip down to pay a visit to the little girls' room and you unpack and I'll see you downstairs in half an hour or so. Oh. No watch," she reminded herself. "Clock on the bedside table there. Take your time." And she was gone back down the stairs.

Jason sighed and put the case and bag on the bed. He walked over to the window and looked out. It was a fine view. To the left he looked up the Dovey valley along the old Roman Road and to the right he could just see the town. The main road ran right outside the house and over the road was a little park. He could see a couple on one of the benches enjoying the view.

He opened the case and began to unpack. He had very little and put pretty much everything in the bottom drawer of the wardrobe. He emptied the bag and put his comics, heavily read on the journey, together with his atlas on the bedside table.

He was about to shut the case when he found a note and opened it. It was from his Mum. *"Dear Jason, I hope you have arrived safely. I've asked Aunt Hettie to give you a little pocket money every week. Don't spend it all at once. Be good to your aunts and Uncle Jack. I miss you already. Love, Mum X."* A pound note was pinned to the note. He smiled and put both the note and money in his pocket. A lump formed in his throat which he fought back.

He did miss his Mum. His home. His room. His stuff. But he would make the best of it – it wasn't forever and being the centre of attention so far it wasn't as bad as he thought.

He gripped the note in his pocket, closed the door behind him and went downstairs where, passing the kitchen, he saw that it was a hive of activity.

"It's only sandwiches on a Saturday but tea's on the go; find yourself a spot in the parlour," Hettie said directing him to the lounge.

As Jason expected tea was a sumptuous affair of sandwiches - egg, cheese, cucumber and salmon - with toasted teacakes and slices of Battenberg cake. Simple, Jason thought, but very effective.

Over tea the subjects of conversation ranged from the tourists in the town, the wonderful job Mrs Thatcher was doing as Prime Minister, the cost of fruit and vegetables to chapel sermons.

This last topic seemed to raise the greatest force of feeling and was high on the agenda. With it being Sunday the next day the chapel service was a highlight of the week for Hettie and Maud, less so for Agnes, and Jack. Emily seemed to be ambivalent towards the event.

"It's important," Maud said banging her cup onto the saucer, "it should set the tone for the week!"

"I think it should be reflective, more in tune with the events of the week," Hettie said.

"As long as it's not too verbose and less of the blood and thunder," Jack said.

"...or boring!" Clarrie added.

There was general agreement that the preacher should ensure that everyone stayed awake and that the service was relevant, and the conversation began to drift onto other, less important matters.

As the evening darkened the curtains were closed and the passing cars on the road became less and less. Much to Jason's surprise the television was not even switched on although it was Saturday night. Instead the room was filled with conversation with Jack and Maud both ensconced in their books and Maud occasionally looking over the top of her reading glasses and tutting at a comment made or an opinion passed.

Jason picked up a large book that Jack had been reading; a glossy photo book of places around the world. He took time to view the photographs of rain forests, cities, mountain ranges and oceans - the colours and character of planet Earth.

30

Soon he started to become drowsy and Maud noticed that he could hardly keep his eyes open. "Come on young man; you've had a long day. Off to bed I think with you."

Jason agreed without argument and kissing each one of his aunts he bid them goodnight. He came to Jack who shook his hand warmly.

"Wonderful to meet you Jason. I bid you farewell and anon," he said. Jason smiled at Jack's flowery sentiment and then bidding everyone a communal "goodnight" he climbed the stairs to bed.

Within a few minutes he was undressed and in an old t-shirt and his underpants, jumped into bed and turned off the light.

The room was lit by a dim orange glow from the streetlight below, with an occasional beam of light scanning the ceiling from a passing car. Jason felt tired, safe and warm and soon was fast asleep.

At about one in the morning he was woken with a start. He switched on the light and looked around the silent room. He felt sure he had heard something but couldn't place what it was; in his sleep it had sounded like a shout or a scream; a cry in the night which he could not explain.

He heard some movement on the floor below him and a quiet, calm voice and decided whatever it had been it was now under control. He turned off the light and was soon asleep for the second time.

4. Meeting thy Maker

Corinthians 13-11
When I was a child, I talked like a child,
I thought like a child, I reasoned like a child.
When I became a man,
I put the ways of childhood behind me.

A t seven the next morning Jason was awoken from a sound sleep by a knock on his bedroom door.

"Good morning Jason." It was Hettie. "Chapel is at eight o'clock. You need to be washed and dressed in your Sunday best. Now, come on! Shake a leg!" He got out of bed and put on his school clothes and tie. He had been warned that he would need these for Sundays and went to the kitchen.

"No breakfast until we're back," Maud said bustling about.

A slamming door broke the Sunday-morning silence as Jason and his aunts, dressed in their church best, walked down the damp steps for the short walk to the Methodist Chapel in the centre of town.

Over the estuary on the Borth side the sun was desperately pushing through the clouds, which drifted lazily atop the distant mountains whilst the tolling of the chapel bell began its call.

As they walked along the High Street others joined the morning walk to church. Jason wondered if they were as hungry as he was; his aunts forbade eating before church – they said it concentrated the mind and made the late breakfast all the more welcome when they got home after the service.

The simple double oak doors were wide open when they arrived and the Reverend Pastor Bryn Evans greeted each warmly.

Maud introduced Jason and the pastor looked down at the boy and smiled. "Pleased to meet you Jason, on this beautiful morning!"

"And you sir," Jason answered politely as his aunts ushered him inside and he was given a Bible and a black dog-eared hymn book.

The aunts took their usual pew close to the front so that Emily, who's hearing was failing, could hear the text and sermon. The chapel was very simple, a small gallery at the back, a few plaques on the walls, a simple wooden cross on an altar and a small church organ, at which, much to his surprise, his Aunt Agnes was sitting. She smiled and then winked at him. Maud scowled as if this was most indecorous behaviour on a Sunday.

At eight o'clock precisely the single bell toll ceased and the doors were closed.

Jason looked around to the congregation behind him and was surprised to see that the chapel was almost full. He also realised that his great-uncle was missing.

He turned to Aunt Clarrie, "Uncle Jack?" he asked.

Clarrie shook her head and whispered, "I'll explain later. Nothing to worry about."

Jason shrugged and fidgeted with the hymn book. He recognised many from his school assemblies. He noticed that the hymn numbers for the morning service were on a board and he looked them up in his book.

Then Jason saw the pastor walking to the pulpit and as if on queue everyone stood.

"Good morning everyone. We'll sing hymn number 27, 'Praise My Soul the King of Heaven'." Aunt Agnes played a verse and the congregation broke into song.

Jason loved the hymn and he found he had a strong voice and that, much to his surprise, he was enjoying himself.

The moment came for the sermon. The Reverend Bryn-Evans had chosen as his theme "Growing" and Corinthians 18 (When I was a child...") as his text.

The sermon was not as painful as Jason was expecting and he actually found himself considering the points the Parson had made.

During the final hymn, 'Jesu Lover of my Soul' the sun burst through the clouds and beamed through the simple stained-glass window creating coloured patterns on the wooden chapel floor. As the hymn ended Jason noticed Reverend Evans smiling at the way the sun and colours had brightened the chapel.

After the blessing Aunt Agnes burst into 'Widor's March' during which the congregation filed from the chapel. As each passed the door their hand was shaken vigorously by the Reverend, whose smile could brighten the darkest of days.

Jason shook his hand and the Reverend looked down at the boy. "Wasn't the sunlight through the window truly uplifting? The Lord creates a wonderful light show does He not?" Jason nodded. "Please give my warmest greetings to your uncle," the Reverend said.

Finally the organ became silent and Agnes appeared carrying a bundle of sheet music, and the Hughes girls walked back through the town to Bryn-Helig.

The sun was beginning to warm the streams and it was noticeably busier with tourists beginning to arrive for the day.

Agnes popped into the paper shop and bought a copy of the Sunday Times and bought Jason a copy of the Record Mirror.

"It's what you young folks read I understand," she said handing it to Jason.

Jason thanked her but didn't have the heart to tell her he'd never read it before and never usually had the money to buy it.

He glanced at the cover picture of Marc Bolan and David Bowie, rolled it up and put it under his arm.

The short walk from the chapel was soon over and the front door was opened to music and the smell of cooking bacon.

Clarrie smiled and shouted, "Jack? You're up!" and entering the kitchen they found Jack standing over the range cooking a pan full of eggs.

"Time I cooked a full English for everyone!" Jack said pointing at his sisters with an egg flipper.

The dining room table was already laid and as they took their seats Jack arrived with trays of egg, sausage and bacon.

"What a surprise!" Agnes said, "Whatever brought this on?"

"Thought you'd welcome it after singing your lungs out," Jack said placing a large rack full of toast on the table and taking his seat.

Maud and Jack glanced at each other as if there was another reason and didn't wish to share or pursue it.

The breakfast was hot and delicious and Jack had cooked enough for an army.

"I thought we could take a walk before lunch along the Old Roman Road," Clarrie said, "Who's up for it?"

"Me," Jason said.

"And me!" both Jack and Agnes added.

"Good! We could take the camera too!" Clarrie said.

Later that morning, with the sun burning off the morning mist, Jason and Clarrie led by Jack, waited for a gap in the stream of traffic and crossed the busy road to the jetty and small park with its wall that looked out over the Dovey estuary.

They walked through the park and through a kissing gate onto what looked like polished granite rocks along the water's edge.

"Treacherous in wet weather but fine in the sunshine," Jack called leading the way.

The path hugged the coastline and Jason looked down to see that much of it was paved and any gullies in the stone had been bridged.

"Been here nearly two thousand years. The Romans used to come up here for shellfish, oysters, mussels and the like and crabs and fish. Very busy place in those days," Jack called a few yards from the front.

Suddenly Clarrie called to stop and she set up a photo of Jack and Jason with the river in the background. Then Jack took hold of the camera and did the same for Clarrie and Jason. His hands seemed to shake a little as he did so.

"Take your time Jack," Clarrie said, "just click the button on the top."

After the photos were taken she swung the little Praktika Camera over her shoulder and they set off again. Turning a corner the banks of the river were pink and purple with flowering rhododendrons.

"How wonderful!" Clarrie exclaimed, "The sun has brought them all out," and she set to work snapping away.

"Now don't waste your shots," Jack warned her, "you know how Maud gets if we have to throw prints away." But Clarrie was undeterred and she set about taking close-ups of the bees on the flowers.

After a short while they finally came to what seemed a natural break in the path where a small fenced jetty stuck out into the river. They walked onto it and shared a strategically placed bench to take in the sunshine and the view. They each took a satisfied sigh.

"Very good for the soul. Better than that religious nonsense, eh Jason?" Jack said teasingly.

"Was that why you weren't at chapel this morning?" Jason asked.

Clarrie's smile left her for a moment and then Jack replied, "No no, my boy. Just felt a little under the weather. Much better now after that breakfast."

"It was very substantial!" Jason said.

"We don't have that every morning," Clarrie said, "Usually just cornflakes and egg. Not in the same bowl of course," and she laughed and put her hand across her mouth to stifle it.

Jack joined her and then said jokingly, "Such indecorous behaviour young lady. And on a Sunday as well!" then after slapping his knees he rose, took a deep breath of salty air and said, "Come on back to Ty Angylion! Maud and Hettie will have the roast on I dare say."

Sure enough at around 2:30, a traditional roast, vegetables and all the trimmings were served. As if this wasn't enough after the cooked breakfast, an apple crumble and custard was brought out to "ooohs" and "aaahhhs" from the table.

After half an hour of small talk around the table everyone, including Jason, pitched in to clear up and within twenty minutes the kitchen and dining room were cleared.

Agnes settled down with the Sunday Times with its many supplements and Jason dipped into each of the ones she didn't want to read or had read, including the sports pages and, for some unknown reason, the business pages.

As the afternoon wore on Jack, Maud and Hettie disappeared for a "lie down" and Emily began snoozing in the chair.

Jason noticed a cool breeze and realised the noise from the front of the house was louder. He guessed the front door was open and got up to investigate.

Sure enough it was and there on the granite step was Clarrie, sitting on a thick cushion with her eyes closed, leaning against the doorframe sunning herself.

Jason returned to the lounge and sat down on the seat built into the bay window. To the one side was a pair of binoculars and he spent a good while watching the birds and boats on the river and the cars on the beach at Ynslas and Borth.

Soon he too closed his eyes and when he opened them again realised he had slept for half an hour. By then it was nearly six o'clock and a few sandwiches were served.

Over tea Maud announced that the TV would be switched on tonight. At first Jason was excited, then Jack nudged him and said under his breath "Songs of Praise" and the excitement wore off very quickly.

Luckily it was left on for "All Creatures Great and Small" which Clarrie had convinced Maud was about hymns rather than a vet's practise in Yorkshire.

Not long after Jason was having difficulty keeping his eyes open and he said his good nights and made the long climb to bed. The room was a little stuffy so he opened the window a few inches to let some air in.

He was going to make a start on the 'Record Mirror' but with tiredness overtaking him he pulled the heavy quilt over himself and closed his eyes. As he drifted away he thought he could hear the distant sound of a gentle sobbing in the night.

5. Theatricals

"What you do still betters what is done.
When you speak, sweet, I'd have you do it ever:
When you sing, I'd have you buy and sell so."

William Shakespeare

*J*ason rose relatively late for breakfast on the Monday morning of his first week to find his aunts already dressed and preparing for some ladies-only meeting which Jason was told firmly that he would be bored rigid by.

They were taking the train to Machynlleth and meeting 20 other ladies at the hotel for coffee.

"Never been to Machynlleth!" Jason said. "Stopped there on the train of course."

"Don't worry Jason, we'll take you over some time soon – I'll get the car out and we'll make a trip," Maud said.

Uncle Jack appeared. "You'll not be missing anything Jason! The restaurants close at lunchtime in Machynlleth." Jason laughed.

After much buzzing about with hats and coats and scarves being taken off and put back on a few times all were happy with their choice of outdoor wear.

"Come on girls or we'll miss the train!" Hettie said and the scurried from the house leaving Jason and Jack waving them off from the front step.

"Anon, anon sisters!" Jack shouted after them.

They closed the door after them and Jack said, "Come on lad, let's see what's to do. Follow me!" and led Jason into the dining room.

"Now wait here!" Jack said and disappeared up the staircase reappearing not long after carrying two large thick books.

"What do you know about Shakespeare?" Jack asked dumping the heavy load on the dining room table.

"William Shakespeare?" Jason said.

"Yes, William Shakespeare. Most youngsters your age don't even know his first name."

"I'm afraid that's about all I do know, except that he's duller than dishwater of course," Jason added. Jack stood and putting a melodramatic hand to his head said, "Dishwater sir! Dishwater! Tis' not so!" He sat down again and said, "It depends, like dishwater, it depends how much rubbish people throw into it! Now do you know anything he wrote?"

"Ermmmm," Jason thought for while, "Romeo and Juliet? That's the one we did at school."

"Good! Excellent," Jack said, "Any others?"

"What's the one with the skull and the young man in a frilly shirt?" Jason asked.

"Hamlet!" Jack said, "The best. The toughest too. But let's start with an easier one, eh?" and he flicked through one of the tomes called 'The Complete Works'.

"How about kings and battles and a bit of romance ter boot?" Jack asked.

"Sounds okay to me," Jason answered.

"I know, help me push the table back and we have the space of the bay window as our stage," Jack suggested and they turned the table round so it gave them about six feet between the bay window and the table. "It sometimes helps standing up to do some of the lines."

"Do you act Uncle Jack?" Jason asked.

"Oh, did once. Long time ago. Started when I was a lad not much older than you. At school."

His voice changed, "I was considered a good actor in my time," he said, "four plays a year from the time I was 13 until I left to join the army at 18. Got through most of the easy ones and a couple of the greats too. King Lear, Hamlet (of course), Much Ado, Richard III and so on and so forth." And he waved his hands vaguely in the air.

"Now. Let's begin. I know, let's share the parts out, you do some and I'll do some," Jack suggested.

"Oh, I don't know Uncle Jack," Jason said, "I'm not very good."

"Away with you. You'll be great. Besides you're amongst friends. And it's Jack. None of this Uncle nonsense."

"Which one are we going to do?" Jason asked.

"Which one? Which one? Oh, of course! 'Henry the Fifth'. Quite short and an absolute masterpiece."

"What's that about then?" Jason asked with a shrug.

"Cabbages and kings! War and peace! Comedy and tragedy! There's even a bit of sissy stuff too."

"But what's the story?" Jason asked beginning to get the thread.

"Well, it follows on from Shakespeare's Henry IV Part 2. Prince Hal's been a bit of a wastrel and layabout. But as soon as his father dies he packs it all in, smartens himself up - even denies his drinking friends - to take up the responsibilities of being the king. The play opens with France threatening the young king with war and Henry declaring war on them. It reaches its climax with the Battle of Agincourt."

"Agincourt? We did that in history! We beat the French!"

"Did we ever! Though I think Bill does massage the facts a little," and Jack tapped his nose. "Now lets begin!" He flicked to Act 1 Scene 1 and with eyes like headlights and a grin like a Cheshire cat, clapped his hands and added, "Oh yes! This is a good bit."

"Mmm. It begins with Chorus, like a narrator, warming up the audience explaining that the theatre was going to be turned into England, France, battlefields and so on and so forth. Tell them the need to use their imagination. No television back then! Come on let's start. I'll do Chorus."

And with a deep breath and eyes twinkling he read the text, his voice like a wizard summoning up the magic through incantation.

"Now!" Jack said, "This is spoken by Chorus; the play's narrator. Imagine him standing as far forward on the stage as you can, arms drawing the audience in." And he began:

> *O for a Muse of fire, that would ascend*
> *The brightest heaven of invention,*
> *A kingdom for a stage, princes to act*
> *And monarchs to behold the swelling scene!*
> *Then should the warlike Harry, like himself,*
> *Assume the port of Mars; and at his heels,*
> *Leash'd in like hounds, should famine, sword and fire*
> *Crouch for employment. But pardon, and gentles all,*
> *The flat unraised spirits that have dared*
> *On this unworthy scaffold to bring forth*
> *So great an object: can this cockpit hold*
> *The vasty fields of France? or may we cram*
> *Within this wooden O the very casques*
> *That did affright the air at Agincourt?*
> *O, pardon! since a crooked figure may*
> *Attest in little place a million;*
> *And let us, ciphers to this great accompt,*
> *On your imaginary forces work.*

Then Jack tapped the side of his nose knowingly and leaned forward towards Jason so he was now no more than two feet away from him:

> *Suppose within the girdle of these walls*
> *Are now confined two mighty monarchies,*
> *Whose high upreared and abutting fronts*
> *The perilous narrow ocean parts asunder:*
> *Piece out our imperfections with your thoughts;*
> *Into a thousand parts divide on man,*
> *And make imaginary puissance;*
> *Think when we talk of horses, that you see them*
> *Printing their proud hoofs i' the receiving earth;*
> *For 'tis your thoughts that now must deck our kings,*
> *Carry them here and there; jumping o'er times,*

Turning the accomplishment of many years
Into an hour-glass: for the which supply,
Admit me Chorus to this history;
Who prologue-like your humble patience pray,
Gently to hear, kindly to judge, our play.

Jason sat transfixed throughout the speech, his eyes as wide as saucers.

"You see, Chorus is saying we've got to tell a story of war and battles and ships and armies and we've only got this limited space to do it in so he's asking the audience to open their minds and use their imagination," Jack said smiling in excitement.

"Yes, I understand. It really comes alive," Jason said.

"Oh yes!" Jack said, "But there's better! But wait, let's read it through and I'll help you. We'll take a part each. You can be Henry of course – I like doing the comic stuff anyway."

And so it was that through the morning they worked their way through the play; occasionally skipping the 'padding' as Jack called it. When they got to the battle speeches Jack helped Jason through them.

"Wait," Jack said, "try that again. Stand up. Here, have this poker as your sword. Now, imagine you are tired, worn out but really angry – the gates are barred against your army; you're a great King, a young man only a few years older than yourself, trying to get his men to lay down their lives and breech the walls of a city yet again. "

Once more unto the breach, dear friends, once more;
Or close the wall up with our English dead.
In peace there's nothing so becomes a man
As modest stillness and humility:
But when the blast of war blows in our ears,
Then imitate the action of the tiger;
Stiffen the sinews, summon up the blood,
Disguise fair nature with hard-favour'd rage;
Then lend the eye a terrible aspect;
Let pry through the portage of the head
Like the brass cannon; let the brow o'erwhelm it
As fearfully as doth a galled rock
O'erhang and jutty his confounded base,

> *Swill'd with the wild and wasteful ocean.*
> *Now set the teeth and stretch the nostril wide,*
> *Hold hard the breath and bend up every spirit*
> *To his full height. On, on, you noblest English.*
> *Whose blood is fet from fathers of war-proof!*

Jason finished the speech and Jack clapped, "Well done my boy! Well done! Worthy of Olivier himself! Oh yes! Very well played!"

It was a defining moment for Jason. It was the first time in as long as he could remember in his short life that anyone had shown such interest in him and he felt a warm glow, which turned into a beaming smile.

"And yes, you should be pleased with yourself," Jack said, "but let's see what happens!"

They continued, to the heights of breeching the walls of Harfleur and the lows of hanging the king's old drinking fellow, Bardolph.

Late in the afternoon, after "skipping the salad of the French princess nonsense to get to the meaty pieces", as Jack said, they reached the Crispin's Days speech.

"Now," Jack said, "you've come all through France, you're cold, wet, hungry and you're outnumbered. Many of your men could die today. You want to tell them they will be remembered no matter what. On you go. Give it a bash!"

Jason took a deep breath and began:

> *We would not die in that man's company*
> *That fears his fellowship to die with us.*
> *This day is called the feast of Crispian:*
> *He that outlives this day, and comes safe home,*
> *Will stand a tip-toe when the day is named,*
> *And rouse him at the name of Crispian.*
> *He that shall live this day, and see old age,*
> *Will yearly on the vigil feast his neighbours,*
> *And say 'To-morrow is Saint Crispian:'*
> *Then will he strip his sleeve and show his scars.*
> *And say 'These wounds I had on Crispin's day.'*
> *Old men forget: yet all shall be forgot,*
> *But he'll remember with advantages*

What feats he did that day: then shall our names.
Familiar in his mouth as household words
Harry the king, Bedford and Exeter,
Warwick and Talbot, Salisbury and Gloucester,
Be in their flowing cups freshly remember'd.

After Jason completed the speech Jack was silent for a few moments, as if moved in some way.

"Well?" Jason said, "OK?"

Jack took a deep breath and composed himself. "More than OK Jason. Excellent." He put his hands on his knees and looked down for a second, perhaps accessing an old long forgotten piece of his past. "The last time I heard that speech outside of a theatre I was standing in an ankle deep of water." He shook his head and sighed, "But that is another story for another day."

He took out his handkerchief and blew his nose.

"Hay fever?" Jason said knowingly.

Jack smiled, "Sure. Hay fever!" He put away the 'kerchief. "Come, let's bring Agincourt to its logical and exaggerated conclusion eh?"

By one o'clock the play was almost done and Jason felt exhilarated. "Shall I do the final Chorus speech?" Jack asked. "Big finish, eh?"

Thus far, with rough and all-unable pen,
Our bending author hath pursued the story,
In little room confining mighty men,
Mangling by starts the full course of their glory.
Small time, but in that small most greatly lived
This star of England: Fortune made his sword;
By which the world's best garden be achieved,
And of it left his son imperial lord.
Henry the Sixth, in infant bands crown'd King
Of France and England, did this king succeed;
Whose state so many had the managing,
That they lost France and made his England bleed:
Which oft our stage hath shown; and, for their sake,
In your fair minds let this acceptance take.

At the end of the speech they both sighed, satisfied with their morning's work.

"So along comes Henry the Sixth and they lose it all?" Jason asked in confirmation of understanding.

"Yes. They ruled most of France and a hundred years later all they had was Calais," Jack replied, nodding his head and he tutted. "Ah well. Ham and mustard sandwich I think for lunch?" and they retired to the kitchen.

After lunch Jack made his apologies and walked up the stairs for his "afternoon ablutions" as he called them. Jason decided he would read his copy of the 'Record Mirror' and followed him up the stairs to get the magazine from his bedroom.

He took it to the lounge and lying on the floor with the sun shining through the bay window he flicked open to the first page.

He scanned some of the headlines to see if there were any bands or artists he'd know about, and to his surprise he did. Marc Bolan and T-Rex were about to tour to promote a new album called *"The Slider"*. He scanned the dates but the closest to where he lived was Birmingham and he tried to imagine himself with the Bolan corkscrew hair.

Alice Cooper was touring to promote *"School's Out"* and was criticised by the watchdogs for using a live snake on stage. He liked Alice Cooper – the eye makeup was particularly weird. Slade were announcing some Christmas dates and were playing the Wolverhampton Civic. Home turf. Now that was more like it! The tickets were way out of his price range but he could dream anyway. Mott the Hoople were playing the Civic as well, supported by some band called Queen. Strange name for a band.

There was a section on progressive music which his mate Stuart liked – he'd even seen Yes at Wolverhampton Civic in October the previous year when they did *Fragile* – they were recording a new album, *Close to the Edge*; Genesis were releasing *Foxtrot* in September and Pink Floyd's sales of *Meddle* could have paid off the country's national debt.

Gradually, during the course of the afternoon he had read half of the paper. He tore out a full-page advert for the Alice Cooper tour with Alice in top hat and leathers with the full makeup in front of a guillotine. He would ask Maud or Hettie if he could put it on the wall but was convinced they wouldn't approve.

He heard the front door slam and a commotion and call from the hall. His aunts were home.

He heard Clarrie call "Jack! Jason!" in her high-pitched voice.

Jason arrived in the hall but there was no sign of Jack; the girls were wielding a few shopping bags. Evidently there had been a visit to the shoe shop.

"We've bought some sensible shoes for walking in. Agnes's bought some slippers and we've bought you some plastic sandals for the beach," Emily said excitedly and taking them from the bag she handed them to Jason. He tried them on and they fitted perfectly.

"We'll give them a test drive in Barmouth in a week or so," Clarrie said, "nothing like a good paddle at the seaside!"

Jason then remembered the Alice Cooper picture and turned to Aunt Maud. "Aunt Maud, I was wondering if I could pin a picture on my wall?"

"Well, I don't know about that, you might damage the wallpaper."

"Oh Maud now don't be daft! That room's not been decorated in ten years. Four holes are not going to make it any worse," Agnes said.

"Please?" Jason asked.

"Please?" Agnes asked of her sister.

Maud smiled weakly; it seemed almost to be an effort, "All right then."

Agnes was already at the bureau and gave Jason the tin of drawing pins and he was off like a shot. He pinned the poster in the empty space above his bed which faced the window. With a satisfied nod he walked down the stairs and was met by Jack as he came from his room on the floor below Jason's.

Jack turned away but Jason caught of glimpse of Jack's reddened eyes. Jack took out a hanky from his pocket and blew his nose hard.

"Damned hay fever; gets me some days," he said and Jason followed him downstairs.

Jack entered the room to shoes being tried on. "Did you get my...?"

"Of course Jack. Cherry flavour as you requested," and Hettie handed over a white package of tobacco.

"One pipe a day! Those were the doctor's orders," Jack said turning to Jason. "Still, what do they know."

"And you know where to smoke it!" Maud reminded him.

Jack rolled his eyes and opening the bureau took an old clay pipe from the drawer and said, "Come on Jason. Let us men find a quiet place to relax and ruminate!"

Jack led him through the front door to the park bench overlooking the estuary in the park.

He dipped into his pocket, charged the pipe bowl with tobacco and taking out an old battered paraffin lighter lit the pipe. It took a few moments to get a steady glow but soon Jack was enjoying the heavy scent of the smoke.

"So my lad, have yer changed yer mind about Shakespeare?" he asked, blowing out a cloud of cherry-scented smoke.

"I think I have," Jason said. "Much more exciting than the way we did it at school."

"Ah, English teachers! What do they know. Told me I would never write but I did," Jack said scornfully.

"You wrote a book?" Jason asked.

"Oh yes! A seminal work on the last years of Beethoven," Jack replied.

"I'm very impressed!" Jason said.

"And so you should be young sir!" Jack said with a smile, digging Jason in the ribs. "Do you know, Beethoven not only composed some of the best music ever written, he was also as deaf as a post and wrote some of the most beautiful love letters to his 'Immortal Beloved'? Took them a hundred years to figure out who she was."

"Who was she?" Jason asked.

"A woman!" Jack said without revealing anything else. "Do you know how he laughed?"

"No?" Jason asked inquisitively.

"Ha, ha, ha, haaaaaaa," Jack said using the first chords of Beethoven's 5th and Jason burst into laugher.

"Do you know any jokes?" Jack asked.

"No. Not me," Jason replied not realising he was wringing his hands nervously.

"Okay. I'll teach you one. The easiest joke in Christendom. Here we go now."

"A man walks into a bar. He goes ouch." Jack paused for dramatic effect. "You would have thought he'd have seen it."

Jason sniggered weakly, "Well I didn't say it was funny did I? I shall make it my mission to teach you a new joke every day you are here but now we shall enjoy the gentle lapping of the waves and the cry of the gulls." And with that they spent the next half hour in silence enjoying the afternoon.

Finally Jack sighed, "Come on lad. We'd better go for tea or Maud will have our wotsits."

"Wotsits?" Jason asked.

Jack thought for a moment, "Yes. Wotsits."

With a shrug Jason followed Jack back to the house.

6. Chores

Corinthians 3: 13-15
Each man's work will become evident;
for the day will show it because it is to be revealed with fire,
and the fire itself will test the quality of each man's work.
If any man's work which he has built on it remains,
he will receive a reward.
If any man's work is burned up, he will suffer loss;
but he himself will be saved, yet so as through fire.

O ver the next few days Jason was kept busy with a number of chores seemingly left for his arrival, ostensibly to keep him occupied.

Initially Jason thought this was an imposition but, since he was told that they would be rewarded at the end of it, he set about his tasks with vigour.

As his work progressed he had wondered whether those rewards would "be in heaven" as Maud suggested or of "remuneration or recompense" as Jack has mentioned. He would plump for the latter rather than the former.

During the morning he had emptied all the bins throughout the house, had put the kitchen peelings on the compost heap in the garden, filled both the kitchen and lounge coal scuttle, taken the newspapers to the cellar and dusted the lounge and dining room.

He'd also been asked to hang out the washing but had made a complete hash of it and had been saved by Hettie's timely intervention before most of it had ended up in a pile on the back lawn. While hanging out the washing he had finally met his Aunts' cat 'Briar', an old brown tabby with long whiskers, a thick coat, piercing green eyes and striking tiger-like markings.

Briar had sat on the garden wall for some time surveying the garden and watching Jason as he attempted to put out the washing. He had that feline look that told you that he thought Jason's efforts were pretty appalling and that his attempts were of the lowest possible standards. He eventually showed his total distain for Jason by hopping off the wall and into the next garden.

Briar was now in his 17th year and kept himself to himself, was apparently rarely seen, sleeping and being fed in the cellar by Emily. He gained entry to the house through the pantry window above the water butt at the side of the house. And for this reason, rain, shine, wind, gale, snow or hail it was always open.

Jason's favourite job was cleaning the brass ornaments. A collection of horse brasses, peacocks, plates, souvenirs from various cities around England and a large Arabian tray which was used as a coffee table next to Jack's chair in the lounge.

They all seemed to tarnish within a few weeks and Jason enjoyed wiping each with an old rag and Brasso cream, waiting for the thin layer of liquid to dull and then polishing them up with a large yellow duster kept for the purpose. Very satisfying, turning dull metal to a bright, mirror-like shine.

Another job was to lay the fire not, as Jason had originally thought, a simple task but one which needed much supervision from Hettie, Maud and Emily all at once. There was apparently the right way to lay the paper waffles on the grate, the kindling on top and a few pieces of coal around and in the kindling.

By mid-afternoon, with chores done and the aunts and Jack lapsing into snoozing or a good book Jason would retire to his bedroom or walk over to the park and throw stones into the sea from the jetty.

One afternoon he arrived back from the park as Jack was just coming down the stairs.

"Ah, the very man! Remuneration I think is called for. Clarrie?" Jack called and she appeared from around the kitchen door.

"Remuneration?" Jack said.

"Remuneration! Yes of course," Clarrie replied, "just two shakes of a lamb's tail!" she added.

She reappeared with a large dark-blue jug, with a chip in the spout which she held in both hands and which at first Jason thought was full of liquid since it seemed to have some weight in it.

"There you go! For all your hard work," Jack said and Clarrie handed the jug to Jason.

In it, filled about halfway was a collection of pennies, two pennies, five pences and a few ten-pence pieces.

"Come on we'll pour it out on the dining room table and count it," Clarrie said.

"Who's it for?" Jason asked.

"For you!" Jack said looking at Clarrie. "We save the odd coin during the year and usually use it for a slap-up meal or afternoon tea or some such but this year we felt you should have some pocket money." Then he winked and whispered, "We'll top it up through your stay though!"

"But what shall I put it in? I don't have a wallet," Jason said.

"I think I can fix that!" Jack said and disappeared.

Jason emptied out the contents on the table and started stacking them into piles of copper and silver. Jack reappeared with some small plastic bags and an old pocket-sized tobacco tin.

"What we'll do is fill the bags up to fifty pence and change them for notes at the bank tomorrow," Jack said, "any silver left you can put in the tin."

Soon four bags had been filled with coppers and another with silver.

"So what's the final figure?" Clarrie asked.

"There is four pounds and seventy pence," Jason said as he placed the seventy pence in the tin. At that moment Agnes came in to see what the clinking was all about.

"Agnes do you have any pound notes?" Clarrie asked.

"A couple I think; Maud may have some in her purse. I'll go and have a look."

She reappeared with a single five-pound note. "Here you are Jason," she said handing him the note.

"But I only have four pounds," he said.

"And now you have five!" Jack said. "Now I'll take the bags of coins to the bank up the road tomorrow and we'll be all square. Well almost. Near enough."

"So what are you going to spend it on?" Clarrie asked.

"I'm not sure," Jason replied, "I hadn't expected to have anything to spend while I was here. I thought of buying a record but I don't have a record player so that would be silly."

Jack glanced at Agnes and then said, "Well you have a good think. We'll be off to Barmouth next week and that tin will be burning a hole in your pocket by then."

Jack smiled and then taking a deep breath said, "Thank you all very much. You're very kind," and he hugged Clarrie and Agnes who were slightly taken aback by this show of affection.

"Thank you Uncle Jack," Jason said, holding out his hand.

Jack shook it warmly and said, "Don't mention it young Jason; don't mention it."

Jason decided to spend an hour or so in his room to read 'Record Mirror' and also to ponder his newfound wealth. He lay on the floor and opened the magazine to the charts pages.

The singles were pretty uninspiring, topped by Donny Osmond, Dr Hook, David Cassidy and the Partridge Family, a sprinkling of soul stars, Bruce Ruffin, Johnny Nash, The Stylistics, The Drifters, Supremes, Roberta Flack and even Michael Jackson had a solo song in the charts.

Most of the glam-rock stars were there including Alice Cooper (*School's Out*), Gary Glitter (*Rock & Roll*), The Sweet (*Little Willy*), T.Rex (*Metal Guru*) of course, and good old Slade (*Take me Back Home*).

His friends, those that had pocket money, had been talking about a new pop star called David Bowie; he had a song called '*Starman*' which he had heard before and thought the album '*Ziggy Stardust*' had a great cover.

He also liked a song by The Who called '*Join Together*' – he could hear the song in his head when he rode his bicycle. He'd seen them once on the TV, the singer had a great voice and the drummer and guitarist were just crazy.

The album charts reflected the single charts with Alice Cooper, David Bowie, and Slade high on the list. He wasn't surprised to see Marc Bolan and T.Rex there with three albums *'Electric Warrior'*, *'Bolan Boogie'* and *'The Slider'* all in the Top 30.

There were a couple of artists, Elton John and Eric Clapton, he hadn't heard of before though his prog-rock mate Stuart had told him Emerson Lake & Palmer were very good.

He realised he was outgrowing the glam rock that had dominated his radio for a few years and though he had some of that music on tapes at home he wanted something more sustainable.

He turned the pages and saw an advert for Uriah Heep's *'Demon and Wizards'* and he admired the artwork and logo.

He thought about the shopping trip into Barmouth, perhaps something would catch his eye but for now he was happy because of his aunts' and uncle's generosity.

He looked at the bedside clock and throwing the paper on the bed realised it was past six o'clock and scurried downstairs just in time for Maud and Hettie serving the tea.

"Come on now Jason, no lolly-gagging!" Maud said, "Up to the table."

Jason nodded a polite "Of course" and joined the others at the dinner table.

7. Shopping

Don't say you don't have enough time.
You have exactly the same number of hours per day
that were given to
Irene Keller, Pasteur, Michelangelo,
Mother Teresa, Leonardo da Vinci,
Thomas Jefferson, and Albert Einstein.

Every Wednesday saw the aunts do their weekly shop; with Jason in the house it was an opportunity for some of the burden of heavy bags to be shared with younger shoulders.

After breakfast, just as Jason was finishing the last slice of toast, Hettie came into the dining room with two bags and two shopping lists. "Now Jason I've done two lists for you," she said. "One is for Jones the Butcher in Church Street and Griffiths the Greengrocer two doors down. There's an old purse. There should be enough money for both shops."

"Come on Jason, I'll walk down with you to get the bits and pieces from the supermarket," Emily announced, "but not too fast a walk, I'm a little slower on my pins these days!"

As they walked from Penhelig down to the town Emily gave him the Cook's tour of Aberdovey. She pointed out the hotel, the old mussel beds, the lifeboat station, the pier and car park then, leaving Jason at the supermarket, she pointed him down Church Street.

Jason entered the butcher's shop and was greeted by the owner, Mr Price Jones, who wiped his hands on a bloody hand towel that Jason was convinced made his hands dirtier than cleaner. Mr Jones proffered him a hand, "I was warned by Miss Hughes you was coming to see us. You got a list I understand."

Jason took out one of the lists from his pocket. Price Jones laughed, "No good here my boy, we don't sell potatoes and leeks!"

Jason rummaged through his pocket for the correct list and handed it over to the butcher.

"Now that's all right isn't it. Let's see what we have here. Bacon, sausages, lamb's liver and pork roast for Sunday lunch. You'll eat well up at the Angel House don't you!" Price Jones said.

"Angel House?" Jason said.

"Yes; that's the English for the house name isn't it – 'Ty Angylion' – the hill behind is Bryn Angylion so that's why they named the house. Did you not know?"

"No, I hadn't been told," Jason said, "it's quite a good name."

"Oh, yes. All those old dears living together. And only one wedding ring amongst them and that was your grandmother," Price Jones said, all the while slicing, weighing and wrapping.

"Now I've given you a good pork joint with extra fat and skin on it; I know how Jack Hughes likes his crackling." He handed over the packages, which Jason packed in his bag.

"Well now that was easy enough wasn't it? I understand you're off to Griffiths now. Turn left and two doors down. He's off to Aberystwyth today – meeting his friend if you know what I mean," and he tapped his nose. "You'll meet Mrs Gwen Griffiths, lovely woman." He sighed, "I was too late there I was. Oh well, mustn't sob over spilt milk."

Jason turned left into the greengrocers and was met at the door by a sturdy woman in her fifties. "Jason. The Hughes' grandnephew if I'm not mistaken," Gwen Griffiths said.

Jason nodded and shook her hand. "I've got most of your things ready. Maud usually has a standing order but let me just check your list."

She took a pencil from behind her ear and ticked off the items on the list.

"Wait a minute. She's got bananas here. She must be doing a trifle I dare say. Oooh, you'll like a good trifle. You might not get the sherry though!" she said and helped Jason pack the second bag.

"There you are my lovely. Two bags and I've balanced them out for you."

Jason paid and left to meet Emily at the bench by the Dovey Hotel. where she was already waiting for him.

"Well it looks as if you're loaded there," Emily said. "Now I've had a good rest we can go back home." And they made their way back along the main road towards the house.

"Mr Price Jones told me the English name of the house – 'Angel House'. It's a beautiful name," Jason said.

"Oh, yes. You might not know this but your great-grandfather built the house with his brother. They helped build the railway and all the bridges and tunnels from Machynlleth to Towyn – even the tunnel behind the house under the hill. They had stone left over and that's what he built the house from."

"Ah, I understand," Jason said.

"You have a look at the house next door. Half the house is made from what was left, and then they bought cheaper stone to finish it off. All built nearly a hundred years ago of course."

As they passed the mussel beds on the seafront they noticed the end cottage was for sale.

"It's been a holiday home for a few years. What a waste," Emily said.

"Looks nice," Jason said peeking through the window, "it looks empty too. No furniture."

"Interesting…" Emily said, "well perhaps a good time to sell. Lots of people passing through in the summer."

"Funny name – Brin-Hell-Ig," Jason said with a very poor Welsh accent.

"Bryn Helig," Emily said correcting his pronunciation, "Helig Hill" she said, "in English."

With a cool breeze blowing off the estuary, they walked back to "Ty Angylion" for a "spot of lunch" as Emily called it.

"I bought some bread rolls and cooked ham at the supermarket," Emily said, "have you ever had ham and mustard sandwiches with mustard strong enough to make your eyes water?"

"No. Can't say I have," Jason replied.

"Well, we'll see what we can do," Emily said laughing.

The mustard was made to Jack's own recipe, apparently made hotter by a dash of white pepper, which cleared the sinuses but was delicious with fresh white bread, butter and thickly-sliced honey-roast ham.

After lunch Jack appeared and said, "I think I may have a little surprise for you."

"Is it what I think it is?" Agnes said.

"Yes, Mrs Wynn at May Bank had an old portable one; it's not working very well but I think I can fix it," Jack replied.

Jason was intrigued and followed Jack and Agnes into the workshop in the cellar. On the work bench was a red box, about 18 inches square, which Jason recognised as a Dansette record player. On the front was a white speaker screen with two white and gold buttons for volume and tone.

"It plays 45s and 33s and I think does old 78s too. The stylus head's a bit loose which made the sound crackly but I've glued it in. Probably won't ever need to buy a new head," Jack said.

"Wow!" Jason said, "It's great! And it works?"

"Yes, well it does now. Hang on we'll test it," Jack said, picking up a single from the bench. "Mrs Wynn found this old Frank Sinatra record she didn't want," and he placed it on the turntable.

The deck started to turn but it sounded like the song was being sung at double time by squirrels on helium gas.

"Ah, should be on 45 not 78 you old fool!" Jack said and they tried again.

The single was a little scratched but played all the same. It was a song called "High Hopes" which Jason had heard on the road and he sang along with the chorus.

> *"He's got high hopes, he's got high hopes.*
> *He's got high apple pie in the sky hopes."*

Agnes and Jack joined in the singing and Jason noticed that their feet were moving and that they were almost, but not quite, dancing.

"Well, I like the lyrics to that one!" Jack said as it finished.

"Let's unplug it and take it up to your room," Agnes suggested and Jack unplugged the record player, put the cable inside the lid, clipped the arm down and handed it to Jason who carrying it like a case took it to his room. There he cleared a space on the dressing table by the window and plugged it into the wall.

"Now remember, it takes a few minutes to warm up," Jack reminded him, making sure it was level.

"And next week we'll go into Barmouth," Agnes said, "I know there's a Woolworth's that sells records and a place for you young people on the harbour too, called Isis."

"But for now I can play Frank Sinatra at least!" Jason said laughing.

"I think I've got a few classical things you could listen to, and we've only a few days and it's off to the bright lights of Barmouth," Agnes said.

"How shall we get there?" Jason asked.

"Well, usually we take the train," Agnes replied, "it's a nice ride up the coast."

"We could hire a little runabout from Pugh's Garage. What do you think?" Jack asked. "Depends how many want to avail themselves of Barmouth's splendour. I know, I'll price it up."

With that they elected to walk out to the park passing Clarrie on the step as she prepared for her afternoon nap in the sunshine. Today was so warm she'd found an old straw hat to cover her eyes and shade her face from the sun.

"It's a beautiful day!" she said as they passed, Agnes carrying her book, Jack with newspaper, tobacco and pipe and Jason with his now battered copy of the Record Mirror.

"Gorgeous! A hot one! Bright and beautiful!" they all agreed and set themselves up around the bench with Jason on the grass.

The afternoon passed into early evening, mostly in silence broken only by the sound of the sea lapping against the harbour wall or the distant cry of a seagull practising dives over the water.

It was, in all, a perfect afternoon.

8. Sensible Shoes

Hebrews 13:2
"Do not forget to entertain strangers,
for by so doing some people have entertained angels
without knowing it."

ithout realising it Jason had been at Ty Angylion for two weeks and in retrospect the time had flown by; he had done and learned much. Maud and Hettie had taught him how to clean, polish and even how to poach eggs.

He'd taken to making his own cooked breakfast specially concocted for him by Emily with boil-in-the-bag breakfast. This involved an afternoon spent cooking beans and grilling tomatoes, mushrooms, bacon and sausage. A serving of each dropped into a freezer bag with the tomato juice and then frozen. Whenever Jason wanted to he could take out a bag from the freezer and drop it in boiling water and have his breakfast made as if by magic.

Jack had educated him in Shakespearean verse that, as a 13-year old, he could have found deadly dull. In fact he actually enjoyed walking through the plays with Jack and doing all the parts and silly voices.

They were apparently saving the biggies (Hamlet, Richard III and King Lear) until last. But Jack had already caused quite a stir on a slightly windy day by standing in the park with his walking stick waving in the air and pointing at a single cloud in an otherwise azure blue sky and reciting Lear's speech spoken in the storm on the heath:

Blow, winds, and crack your cheeks! rage! blow!
You cataracts and hurricanes, spout
Till you have drench'd our steeples, drown'd the cocks!

"Uncle Jack!" Jason shouted when Jack was in mid-flow but Jack continued like the storm – unabated:

You sulphurous and thought-executing fires,
Vaunt-couriers to oak-cleaving thunderbolts,
Singe my white head! And thou, all-shaking thunder,
Strike flat the thick rotundity o' the world!
Crack nature's moulds, all germens spill at once
That make ingrateful man!

At this point Jason suggested that Jack should stop but he was now in full flow.

Rumble thy bellyful! Spit, fire! spout, rain!
Nor rain, wind, thunder, fire, are my daughters:
I tax not you, you elements, with unkindness;
I never gave you kingdom, call'd you children,
You owe me no subscription: then, let fall
Your horrible pleasure; here I stand, your slave!

This all came as a shock to a number of weekend walkers who thought that perhaps Jack had been given a day out from a nearby retirement home.

Jack took a deep breath, "Ah! That was good! Haven't done that for years. I could have ba'heen han Ak-Tor," he said stretching and annunciating every syllable.

"Shall we get some lunch?" Jason asked expectantly.

"A capital idea. Sustenance. Vitals. Mead. Sack. Food!" and Jack signalled Jason to follow where Hettie made them thick mustard-and-ham sandwiches, which threatened to burn Jason's eyeballs.

After lunch Jack took to this bed for his afternoon siesta and it was at this time Jason always wondered what he was going to do for the rest of the day.

One such afternoon, after a particularly fine lunch, the aunts decided to "test drive" their sensible shoes and walk to the top of Bryn Angylion, the Welsh granite hill which rose behind the house.

Jason was given a battered canvas rucksack to carry, which he assumed contained a flask and suitable sustenance for the outing.

The walk was not a long one, no more than an hour, but the climb to the top could be taxing for the unprepared. The path started by following the old Roman road then, before the jetty, it doubled back under a bridge and up on the other side of the main road into a quiet wood.

As the sun was particularly hot they were thankful for the shade of the trees. The path climbed gradually until it came to a kissing gate followed by a stile over a mossy granite wall.

Soon they were clear of the wood and following sheep tracks potted with craters and strewn with slate chips.

They appeared from behind a rise in the hill and came to an old weather-beaten metal bench, which had a panoramic view up the estuary towards Machynlleth and down the estuary out to the sea.

"On a clear day I'm sure you can see Ireland," Clarrie said catching her breath and slumping onto the bench.

"Ireland?" Jason laughed, "On a day like this I wouldn't be surprised if you could see New York!"

"What stuff and nonsense," Maud said, "as if. You can hardly see Borth and the other side."

Agnes nudged her sister in the ribs. "I think they're joking."

After a short rest they climbed the final stretch to the top of the hill where they found a huge concrete stand with a plinth topped with a brass triangulation point.

The block was sheltered from the slight breeze and they made themselves comfortable sitting on their coats.

"Now young Jason. Open up your knapsack!" Hettie ordered.

Jason unzipped the bag and found a flask with ready-milked tea, which he passed to Hettie, a Tupperware box of cheese-and-pickle sandwiches, a few bags of plain crisps, a can of cola for Jason and a large bar of Cadbury's Fruit and Nut chocolate.

Almost in silence - for nothing needed to be said which could have made the experience more enjoyable - they tucked into the sandwiches and crisps and enjoyed the clean air, the grass, the sunshine, the peace and the view.

Then Hettie took the bar of chocolate and broke it into five large pieces for the perfect snack.

"Simple, but effective," Agnes said.

"Yummmm," Clarrie said finishing off her chunk of chocolate.

Having finished they each began to get up and stretch.

"Should be getting back," Hettie said as Jason helped her up.

Clarrie rose and wobbled on her feet almost falling over but stopped herself on the plinth.

"Oopps, a buttercup," Clarrie said opening and closing her eyes, "must have got up a little too quick."

"Are you all right?" Maud asked.

"Oh, yes be fine in a moment," Clarrie replied, "come on let's get back home."

"Wait! Wait!" Agnes said, "In the bag. The camera!"

Jason took out the old battered Praktika and the aunts all gathered around the plinth.

He took a photo of them and then Clarrie took one of him with the other aunts.

"A souvenir," she said putting the lens cap on and for a moment they all just stood and enjoyed the spectacular view.

They began the descent, which of course was much quicker, and within half an hour they were back on the Roman road and in the park where they found Jack having a constitutional smoke of his pipe.

"So! How were the sensible shoes?" Jack asked, and there was general agreement that they had been broken in.

Back at the house tea and biscuits were brought out then everyone disappeared to their rooms for a nap, including Jason who frankly hadn't walked such a distance for some time.

Lying on the bed he realised that he hadn't thought of home for some days. Perhaps later he would write to his Mum he decided, and was soon dozing on the bed.

9. Barmouth

Corinthian 3:18
Let no man deceive himself.
If any man among you thinks that he is wise in this age,
he must become foolish,
so that he may become wise

Finally the day arrived that for some weeks they had all been waiting for: the summer trip into Barmouth. Jack had researched renting a car but given that everyone wanted to go it was decided that they would take the train – no more than an hour's travel.

"And the trip is all along the coast. Very scenic," Emily said.

"And you can read your book too!" Hettie said teasing her.

They also elected not to take a picnic but have a light lunch somewhere in Barmouth town centre.

At nine o'clock they were all standing expectantly on the wooden platform of Penhelig Halt waiting for the rumble of the train, which had stopped previously at Dovey Junction.

Jason's keen hearing picked it up first, a vibration through the platform and then a gentle rumble coming along the line and through the tunnel.

Finally the two-carriage diesel shuttle appeared from the tunnel's mouth and screeched noisily to a stop.

"They never have steam trains any more!" Jack complained.

"There's been no steam on this line for 10 years!" Maud said.

"Well, I still like the steam trains just the same," Jack said and they all climbed aboard.

The train was quiet and open with plenty of space and they took two sets of seats behind each other on the seaside of the train for the best views.

There was some "kerfuffle" as Hettie called it as the aunts moved themselves around as some didn't like travelling backwards or forwards but soon everyone had settled down reading books, newspapers or most just watching the world go by.

Jason had learned the route off by heart and counted the stations – Aberdovey, Towyn, Fairbourne and Barmouth - and his excitement was growing with each station.

Just outside Towyn Jack opened a bag of humbugs, which were shared out creating a scent of mint throughout the carriage.

After an hour, which passed quickly, the train clattered over the bridge crossing the river at Fairbourne into the town of Barmouth.

The train gave a screech and came to a jolting halt and windows were dropped to open the doors.

Jason helped each of his aunts off the train onto the platform since there was a little drop and a gap between train and platform.

Immediately Maud led the way from the station and into Barmouth which had the air of a bustling seaside town with souvenir shops hung with beach balls, rubber rings and little dinghies.

Their first stop was to the "Maybank Tea Shop" which was owned and run by a couple who had once lived a few doors up from the Aunts in Aberdovey.

They were greeted with waves and hellos from behind the counter.

"Good morning Mrs Evans!" Hettie called, "Five teas, one coffee and a cola I think."

"Right away Hettie," Mrs Evans, a roly-poly rosy-cheeked lady, said. "I'll bring over a selection of biscuits too!"

The group took over a couple of tables in the window so they could watch the people out on the street.

The day was a little overcast but warm just the same with a brisk breeze coming off the sea.

The drinks arrived and were consumed eagerly while each discussed their plans for the day.

It was at this point Jason realised that he was going to be allowed to go off to 'cry havoc' about the town as Jack said. Jack reached behind him and picked out a tourist map and opened it on the table in front of Jason.

"Now young adventurer. We are here." He took out a pen and circled the café with his pen on the map. "And there's the station where we've come from. I suggest you go off for a couple of hours – do your own thing - as you young people say and we meet at the Waterside Restaurant for lunch at say one o'clock." He took out his pocket watch and added, "Let's synchronise watches."

For a moment Jason looked lost.

"Ah! You don't have a watch do you?" Jack remembered, and he dipped his hand into his jacket pocket and pulled out an old watch and handed it to Jason with great ceremony.

Jason examined it wide-eyed; it had a brown leather strap and a square gold face with roman numerals. It showed the time as three minutes past eleven.

"It was mine but I can't wear it any more," Jack said, "the strap is too fiddly."

"Thank you very much," said Jason and as he put it on his wrist said, "I'll be sure to look after it and give it you back before we get back on the train."

Jack laughed and slapped his knees as he always did when surprised, "I'm not lending it you Jason! It yours. To keep. Doing no one any good gathering dust in my dressing table drawer!"

Jason couldn't believe Jack's generosity, "Thank you Uncle Jack. Many, many thank yous!"

"Now!" Jack said, "As procrastination is the thief of time and time and tide wait for no man, you should get on your way." And they walked from the café leaving Maud to settle up.

"I'm going to the hotel to meet an old soldier friend of mine – he's come down from Porthmadog to see me so I'm going to the right and you," and he pointed towards Woolworths "might want to go that way."

Jason waved and shouted, "Thank you – at 1 o'clock"

"Adieu and anon!" Jack shouted back.

Jason headed to the left and went straight into Woolworths and found the music department. At first he was disappointed in their selection of 'Best of', 'Top of the Pops' and 'Greatest Hits' albums, most of which were covers, not by the original bands.

None of the songs in the singles charts attracted him and he was about to leave when the assistant pointed him to the half-price box on the counter.

He flicked through the singles and found a copy of *'Join Together'* by the Who which he thought was a great song and priced at 45 pence was a bargain. As he checked it for damage he realised the centre was missing.

"Excuse me," he asked the assistant, "the centre is missing to this record? Do you have another?"

"Ah, no problem lovie," the girl said and found a little black star-shaped circle which she clipped into the middle, "there you are! All set!" she said putting the single into a little plastic bag.

Jason nodded and took out his tobacco tin and paid with a 50 pence piece.

"Thank you," he said then asked, "Do you know any other record shops in the town?"

"There's one but that just sells classics and musical instruments. Now wait. If you go to the harbour, over the road and straight on, you'll find a shop called 'Isis' – it does all sorts including records down there."

Jason thanked the girl and followed the directions. At the harbour front he found a few tacky souvenir and gift shops, a chipper and the last in the row was a wooden-fronted shop called 'Isis'. He opened the door to be engulfed by a smell of incense, Nag Champa and patchouli.

"Morning," a young man, a student doing holiday work, said, "have a look around."

The shop was crammed with crystals, stones and incense. The ceiling was hung with T-shirts and kaftans and fantasy posters by Roger Dean and Rodney Matthews hung on the walls. A stick of incense burnt lazily on the counter.

In the corner he found the record selection and began to flick through – Camel, ELP, Focus, Genesis, PFM, Pink Floyd and Yes.

There was something about Yes, the logo, the sleeve, the positive name which attracted him and which seemed to sound a chord. At the front of the selection was the album '*Fragile*'. He picked it up and examined the record's sleeve and track list. Inside the sleeve was a booklet, which he took out to see that it contained information about each band member. Within a few moments he had made his unequivocal selection: Yes – '*Fragile*' and he took the record to the counter.

"Oh, good choice!" the young man said, "These guys are making quite a name for themselves. Saw them in London at the Speakeasy."

"Yes, my friend saw them at the Civic in Wolverhampton last year," Jason replied.

"Have you heard this?" the man asked.

"Well, no I haven't," Jason replied.

"Look, we're not busy at all. Why don't I make us a squash and we'll have a listen to it!" the student said, and offered Jason a hand. "Steve, Steve Norfolk. University of Lancaster, " he said.

"Jason. Jason Hughes," Jason replied and Steve disappeared and reappeared with two large pint glasses of orange squash and some custard cream biscuits.

He dusted off his hand and opened the Perspex top of the record player. He took the record from the sleeve, put it on the player and as it got up to speed he placed the stylus on the record.

He stood back and tweaked the volume and an acoustic guitar chord, bright and loud, escaped from the speakers and reverberated around the shop.

"Opening track this is, called '*Roundabout*'; written in the back of a bus going around the roundabouts of Aberdeen apparently, by guitarist Steve Howe and lead singer Jon Anderson," Steve explained.

"Are they Scottish?"

"Nah, English. This is their fourth album – got this new keyboard player Rick Wakeman. He replaced the old one, Tony Kaye. Rick's a bloody genius – mental of course but a genius. Plays on Bowie's '*Life on Mars*' you know."

Jason shook his head and they listened intently to the track with Steve playing air guitar, air drums and air keys.

The track finished with a flourish and Steve gave a shriek of "baaaaaannnnggg!" on the final note and added "'...ucking brilliant".

"Now, each band member's done a solo track - this next track is by Rick – it's his version of the 4th Symphony by Brahms."

This segued into Jon Anderson's amazing *'We Have Heaven'* with overlay upon overlay of vocal harmonies.

"What's he singing?" asked Jason.

"I think its 'Tell the moon, don't tell the March Hare ...'" Steve scratched his head, "... it's a word painting apparently," he added nodding his head.

"Oh," said Jason trying to understand the concept.

Then the album went into a frenetic long track called *'South Side of the Sky'*. "Oh yes, I like this one!" Jason said nodding his head in time to the music.

With Side One finished Steve flipped the album over to Side Two and they were treated to *'Five Per Cent for Nothing'* – "it's about what the management gets!" Steve said and Jason laughed.

Then *'Long Distance Runaround'* and Chris Squire's track *'The Fish'* with its growling bass in which Jason could see the woofer speakers almost bounce out of the speakers on the wall.

All the while Jason was examining and re-examining the cover with its beautiful Roger Dean artwork of fragmented planet and wooden ship shaped like a scorpion fish.

"And now the big finish I think," Steve said and they were treated to *'Mood for a Day'* and *'Heart of the Sunrise'* which ended with a snippet of *'We Have Heaven'* again.

"And ... there you are! *'Fragile'* by British rock band Yes. Atlantic Records catalogue number 7211. Marks out of ten please?" Steve asked.

"Definitely a ten! Oh most definitely a ten!" Jason said, gulping back a final slug of orange squash, as Steve gently put the record in the sleeve and the album into a plastic bag.

"We're out of our own bags but I've got this one for a new label called Virgin. The logo's been designed by Roger Dean again – same as the '*Fragile*' cover. And I shouldn't do this but..." and he dropped a post card of the Roger Dean cover into the bag.

"Thank you!" Jason said.

"You're welcome. Broken up a boring morning nicely. If you're ever in Lancaster look me up; I'm usually in the Uni Bar on a Friday and Saturday."

Jason could not imagine how he would ever get to Lancaster or indeed into the bar but they shook hands again and Jason proudly walked from the shop feeling on top of the world.

He looked at his watch and with fifteen minutes to spare walked back to the town centre. Just as he arrived at the Waterside Restaurant he was greeted by Hettie and Maud and moments later a laughing and giggling Clarrie, Jack and Agnes.

"Come on Maud!" Jack said, "We're starving here! Sustenance! Six roast dinners required I think!"

They were obviously regulars and recognised by the waiter. They were given a large table in the window overlooking the harbour and the sea, bay and mountains beyond. Over the hills Jason could see clouds forming and nudged Jack.

Jack looked over the bay, "Yes, we'll get a shower I think. Dramatic when it rolls in off the sea, eh?"

Sure enough as they ate it started raining "like stair rods" as Agnes said and tourists and shoppers took cover in bus shelters and under shop awnings.

Then as quick as it had started the rain stopped and the pavements steamed as the rain evaporated and the sun again shone down on the holiday town.

The afternoon was spent doing "bits and pieces" for the house – a new hand brush, some hand towels and curtain rings – and soon they were standing on the platform again waiting for the train to take them back. Clarrie was sitting on a bench leaning against Emily and Agnes. Jack was smoking his pipe and Maud and Hettie were gossiping about the noise and general behaviour of the tourists.

On the train everyone seemed to doze, including Jason. Soon they were walking from Penhelig Halt and were unlocking the front door of Ty Angylion.

Maud stretched, "I fear tea will be soup and sandwiches tonight!"

"If I'm still awake to eat it," Jack said.

"I'm going for a lie down," Clarrie said and Emily and Agnes followed suit.

"Come on Jason," Hettie said, "looks like we've got some energy left. Let's make up some sandwiches. You butter the bread and I'll slice some cheese and tomatoes. "

So Jason and Hettie made a plate of sandwiches ready for tea. They opened a large bag of potato crisps and Hettie took out a cake tin with an apple cake.

She picked it up and smelt it, "Dorset Apple Cake! Mum's recipe. Never fails." She placed it on a large plate and covered it with a tea towel.

By the time the table was laid out Jack and the aunts were coming wearily down the stairs with "yawns and aaarghs" like sleepy bears.

Tea was consumed and afterwards with the light fading Jack, Agnes and Clarrie crossed the road to watch the sun sink into the horizon in a blaze of reds, oranges and deep corals.

"So? What do think of the day Jason?" Jack asked.

"Perfect I think," Jason said smiling broadly, "pretty much perfect!"

10. Music of the Spheres

Psalm 77:6

I remember my music in the night,
With my heart I meditate, and my spirit doth search diligently:

A fter breakfast the next day Jason returned to his room to finish reading his Record Mirror but more importantly to listen to his new purchases. Throughout the morning the A and B sides of The Who's single were played "to death" and he managed to listen to most of *'Fragile'* twice with a few tracks being skipped so that he could listen to the longer pieces. By late morning even he was getting bored with the repetition of it and Agnes's appearance with a mug of tea and a plate of biscuits was a welcome relief.

"We thought we'd possibly lost you for good to music!" she said walking into his room and placing the plate and mug on the dressing table.

She picked up the album cover and examined it. "What beautiful artwork! And what a very positive name. Mind you, one LP and a single isn't really a collection is it!"

Jason laughed, "I agree – it would be great to listen to more."

"Why don't I fetch a few of mine? They're classical but very listenable and if you've not heard some of the greatest composers it's high time you did." And she disappeared to the next floor reappearing five minutes later with three LPs.

"Now this is the 'Best of Mozart', this is 'Best of Beethoven' and I have a Stravinsky record with one of my favourite pieces on it called the *'Firebird'*. These were all your great-grandfather's. He was very keen on the classics."

"He adored Wagner but listening to the whole of *'The Ring'* would take us a few days. Wagner has his moments but he also has his 20 minuteses." She sat on the bed. "So, which one first?"

Jason thought for a moment, "Perhaps not Wagner. Why don't we start with your favourite; *'Firebird'*?" The piece started very quietly.

"Imagine a phoenix rising from the ashes of a fire; it starts to materialise and then…. takes to the air!" Agnes said excitedly.

A low horn heralded majestic strings until in the mind's eye one could see a beautiful bird appear from the flames, before the music changed to fanfares; a celebration of life and freedom.

Jason's eyes were as wide as saucers. "This was certainly on a par with Yes," he thought and he realised in that moment that his musical horizon had been widened.

"Shall we try the Mozart?" Agnes asked.

"Yes, of course," Jason said making himself comfortable on the floor.

"This first track is the *'Overture'* from *'The Marriage of Figaro'*. Try to imagine the hustle and bustle of a house getting ready for a wedding," Agnes explained.

Jason listened carefully and could hear the excitement, the anticipation, and the activity at a frenetic pace.

"Listen, you can hear the food being laid out, the guests arriving and greeting each other, and the joy of the occasion," Agnes said.

Jason's head bounced along to the music and he found himself smiling at the twists and turns and the 'fun' that he was hearing. The piece finished with a flurry of animated shrills and thrills and Jason found himself clapping as it finished.

"I can see you enjoyed that," Agnes said, "now try this. I won't tell you what it is. Tell me what you hear."

The piece began quietly and slowly with a sad chorus, the vocal bass and sopranos building up to a crescendo of sorrow. Jason tried his best to put into words what he was hearing. He could imagine weeping, wailing, tears and an outpouring of grief. It was one of the most sublime pieces he'd ever heard. "What is it?" he asked.

"It's called *'Confutatis Maledictis'* – it's from Mozart's *'Requiem'*. It was completed after his death – wonderful isn't it?" Agnes explained.

Through the hour before lunch they played most of the Mozart which Jason really enjoyed, then Agnes heard Maud call that it was ten minutes to lunch.

"Let's try a little Beethoven. One of the most glorious pieces every written. Something to whet our appetites! This is the end of his 9th Symphony – some people call it '*Ode for Joy*'."

When the music started Jason could imagine someone running, and running, and running, full of the joy of freedom and happiness. Then the piece changed such that a choir picked up the harmony while the melody continued to weave in and out, all the while building up until it suddenly became quiet and gentle, almost like the calm before the storm, which then came in a thunderous wave of voices and instruments. Jason couldn't understand what they were singing – it was in German - but he could tell they were exhilarated, elated, blissful – in a word joyous. Just when he thought it had ended the music built up again to a wondrous crescendo of happiness and joy.

While Jason listened he hadn't noticed Jack standing in the doorway, smiling at Agnes. He was watching a young boy hearing and discovering Beethoven's 9th Symphony for the first time. It was a coming of age!

At the final verse Jason found himself singing along, conducting the music and on the final note shouting "Yes!!!" at the top of his voice and falling backward on the bed.

"Brilliant!" he shouted, "Brilliant!"

"Don't know anyone who has ever not enjoyed that," Jack said clapping and shouting "More!"

"Well perhaps after lunch," Agnes said taking Jason's hand, "welcome to a bigger world young man!"

And with Jason grinning like the Cheshire cat they walked down the stairs to lunch.

After lunch Agnes and Jason returned to their exploration of the music of the spheres and with the rest of the aunts elsewhere around the house or away on errands Jason set the record player up in the lounge. Occasionally Agnes and Jason would lapse into conversation on subjects outside of music.

"You were married before?" Jason asked.

Agnes smiled and nodded, "Yes. He was a fine man; had a wonderful sense of humour, he adored travel and we saw most of Europe. He had an affinity with Germany, Austria and Switzerland and could speak fluent German. He served as an advisor during the Second World War and when it ended was posted by the government in Stuttgart."

"That's in South Germany?" Jason asked.

"Yes, a couple of hours from France and Switzerland, about four hours drive to Austria. I lived out there with him in his final year and we were married in the following year. Living in sin! That's what father called it – but stuff and nonsense. We loved each other," she said taken back to her halcyon days.

"While we were out there we visited most of South Germany; Rothenburg, Nuremburg, Munich – all of Switzerland – we loved the area around Grindelwald and Interlaken. Oh, wait a moment..." and she reached behind her to the shelf next to the mantelpiece, "here have a look!"

She handed him a little plastic Swiss chalet with a little red chimney. The back of the chalet had an eye piece and when you looked through it and clicked down on the red chimney it showed slides of the countryside, lakes and mountains in the Bernese Oberland.

There were about fifteen images and it looked very green, very sunny and stunning.

"Beautiful!" Jason said handing back the chalet.

"It was; it is," she said, "and if you ever get the chance to go, you must see it." She pointed to the wall at a cuckoo clock. "We bought that in Grindelwald in 1950. Bellows have gone so it doesn't cuckoo anymore so we never set it going. "

The chains were both fully pulled so Jason stood on the chair and set the hands at the right time and set the pendulum swinging. As he did so the cuckoo chimed without a sound.

Agnes smiled, "Nice to see the old thing going at least!"

"What was you favourite place?" Jason asked.

"Well, we loved Switzerland of course, but our favourite city, the city David, my husband, really loved was Salzburg. A very beautiful city – Mozart's birthplace. We managed to get there most years, when we could afford it, to go to the Kristkindel Markt – the Christmas Market – a very romantic place to be around Christmas. It's where he proposed; on the steps of the Dom."

"I think I've seen pictures; it has a castle on the hill – it was where they filmed the Sound of Music!" Jason said.

Agnes laughed; "Yes! One of my favourite films - something else Maud would call stuff and nonsense."

"Well it is a very soppy film with singing nuns!" Jason said wrinkling up his nose.

"Oh I dare say, one day soon – you'll have a girlfriend and be up for 'soppy films'!" Agnes said ribbing him and they both laughed.

The afternoon continued in much the same vein with a young teenager finding enjoyment spending time with an older lady – both had something to give and take from the hours and the time flew by.

"Tell me more about my grandfather," Jason asked.

"Oh, Charles Hughes was a very difficult man," Agnes said, "very difficult. He was unlike his brother and sisters. Very grasping, very brutal – partly because he served in the army during the Second World War as a Captain in the Welsh Regiment, and spent most of his time ordering people about - thought he could do the same when he came home. Your grandmother and he were always arguing; she was a lovely woman and took no nonsense from him."

"How did they die?" Jason asked.

"You don't know?" Agnes said in surprise.

"No my father won't talk about it," Jason replied.

"Oh, the acorn doesn't fall far from the oak! Your father really is his father's son!" she said. "It was in the December of 1955, up near Pwllheli. In a car accident. Your grandfather tried to overtake a queue of traffic and collided head on with a milk lorry. They both died instantly."

"That's perhaps why father won't talk about it," Jason said.

"Mmm, perhaps," Agnes replied.

"Where are they buried? Are they buried in the chapel cemetery?" Jason asked.

"Oh no. Against all our wishes your father wanted them cremated," Agnes said, "he had their ashes scattered in Shell Bay, just up the coast, one of their favourite places apparently."

There was a pregnant pause.

"But why?" Jason asked.

"You father hated his father and sometimes it seemed to us that his life revolved around doing anything he could to go against his father. They had a very strained relationship. At his funeral – it was held at this awful crematorium in Wolverhampton - your father was seemingly inconsolable."

"But why?" Jason asked, "You would have thought that if they didn't get on he would be glad to see him go."

"Ah, you would have thought. I spoke to your Mum about it some weeks later. It turns out that when his father died it was as if all that he had lived for – the hatred of his father – meant that your father no longer had anything to live for. Spent his life proving himself to his father and never gaining the recognition," Agnes explained.

"So, when his father died my father had nothing left to hate and therefore nothing to live for," Jason said and Agnes bit her lip and nodded.

"How very sad," Jason said.

"Isn't it?" Agnes replied. "Even the money that your father inherited didn't seem to count for anything. It's as if he just continues the work that his father had begun."

"It's no wonder he can be very irritable. My mother says it's the stress of his work but I always felt it was something deeper," Jason said. "Well it's a lesson I shall surely not repeat," he added.

"Good lad, break the pattern," Agnes said, and Jason nodded in agreement. "It's always great to see a wise head on young shoulders," she added and kissed his cheek.

11. Letter Home

"The Creator gave you two ears and one mouth.
So you can listen twice as much as you speak"

Jason realised that he was now into his fourth week and after some reminding by Hettie and Maud thought he'd better write to his Mum and Dad and let them know how he was doing.

He thought some time about exactly what he should write and then Emily lent him her letter writing case. Jason unzipped it and found a pad of blue Basildon Bond paper inside and a wodge of heavy-weight envelopes. There was also a black cartridge-ink pen with a gold nib. Jason had written with such a pen before but had tended to cover his fingers with blotches of ink, and often the paper as well,. He sighed and thought he'd have a try and keep his letter neat.

He wrote the address at the top right and beneath it the date and began:

Dear Mum and Dad,

I hope you are both well. I am having a fine time in Aberdovey and the aunts are taking very good care of me.

In fact they are probably spoiling me and have given me a little record player. I have already bought two records with my pocket money. A record by the Who called Join Together and an LP by Yes called Fragile.

Uncle Jack is very good to me and has been teaching me Shakespeare, while Aunt Agnes has taught me about classic music, including Mozart, Beethoven and even Wagner.

The weather here has been fantastic. It's only rained at night so every morning everything is fresh and clean. Most days have been sunny and warm and I've managed to be outside in the park quite often.

Maud and Hettie have been feeding me well and have been teaching me to do chores and I am getting very good at polishing the brass.

Earlier in the week we went to Barmouth which was great fun.

Tomorrow is great-granddad Bill's birthday and we are apparently going to celebrate it in style.

Take Care.

Love

Jason

Jason folder the letter, placed it in a blue envelope, addressed it, and took it straight downstairs.

He found the kitchen in a hive of activity; Maud and Hettie ensconced in the kitchen making strawberry jam. This was an annual occurrence and this year was no exception. A huge copper pot was on the stove bubbling away and jars were being washed, labels and lids prepared.

"We're down to our last few jars so it's about time," Hettie said.

"But strawberries are a terrible price this year," Maud said, "we've done it 30% rhubarb – the rhubarb takes the taste of strawberry."

"Very clever," Jason said smelling the steam from the huge pot. "When will you be able to eat it?"

"A week or so it's usually done," Maud said, "should be all jarred up by tea-time though."

"Aunt Maud, I've written to my parents. Do you have stamp?" Jason asked.

"Surely. Leave it in the rack and it will get posted tomorrow. Second class is alright isn't it?" Maud asked.

In the lounge Jack was doing the crossword puzzle in the newspaper. Out on the front doorstep Clarrie was fast asleep and Emily was snoozing on the sofa, knitting still in her hand.

"Where's Agnes?" Jason asked.

"Popped into town," Jack said, "I think she may be drumming up support for donations to the organ bellows appeal."

Jason took a seat in the window and picked up the binoculars and began picking out the boats on the river and the cars on the beach at Ynslas.

He looked at his watch; it was 15:45 but for the first time in a long while he didn't have a clue what day it was. Days were beginning to merge into themselves and he found his head clearer because of it.

By nine in the evening, having read the newspaper cover to cover, he went to bed and slept easily.

The following day Jason found to his surprise that Jack was up and already eating breakfast. Looking at Jack's plate you could tell it was a hearty double helping.

"Big day Uncle Jack?" Jason asked sitting down at the table.

"Yes, a commemorative one," Jack said.

"Sorry?" Jason asked.

"Years ago I was very ill and the doctor diagnosed a pint of beer a day, plenty of fresh air and walks; I took no notice of the doctor of course who died a few months after having given me the advice but, in his honour, I do a long walk once a year during the summer to commemorate the advice and give thanks that I've lived another year."

"Where do you walk to?" Jason asked.

"Well over the hill at the back – Bryn Angylion – then over the other side to Towyn and then a little way on to Tal-y-lyn. There's a pub there called the Red Dragon where I get a pint and ploughman's lunch. And if I get a move on I should be there by lunchtime."

Jason thought for a moment then asked, "Do you want some company?"

Jack smiled, "Jason much as I enjoy your company on this occasion this is to be a pilgrimage; were it not for the beer it would be a solitary monastic wandering. My annual perambulation!"

"Have I perhaps… ?" Jason ventured.

"No, no, by no means!" Jack said, "Just want to be alone with my thoughts – it can be very cathartic."

He looked at his watch, "Speaking of which, nine o'clock; I should be on my way – need to get some Murray mints from the corner shop afore I go!" he said, and grabbing an old khaki rucksack from by the door, he placed an old tweed peeked cap on his balding head and with a wave as he passed the window was on his way.

Hettie came in with a cup of tea for Jason. "Jack's off on his annual walk," he told her.

"Yes, August the 15th," Hettie said.

"What' so special about August 15th?" Jason asked.

"The day Jack was retired from the army in the First World War. The day he left hospital and came home. He'd been gassed and spent three months in there recovering," Hettie replied.

"Oh," Jason said in reflection.

"Don't worry Jason. He wouldn't have talked about it unless you asked directly," she replied. "He's afraid the dam might burst."

"Dam? What dam?" Jason asked.

"Of emotion. He holds too much back." And she left Jason looking out across the estuary.

12. Lanterns

We shall find peace.
We shall hear the angels,
we shall see the sky sparkling with diamonds.

*T*he following afternoon the aunts and Jack were sitting in the lounge having an after-lunch chat. Jason watched as they talked and interacted with each other. You could see the love between them and he could imagine quite easily how they would have been as children or youngsters.

"Well! Today's the day!" Clarrie said.

"Today?" said Jason.

"Yes! Do you remember your great-grandfather? Your Dad's Dad?" Maud asked.

"I can only remember him hugging me. I remember he had a hug like a bear," Jason replied.

"Yes, he was a big man, taller than your father, over six foot," Hettie said.

"Yes, the kindest..."

"Most generous..."

"Funniest..."

"Yes, funniest!"

"Man," they all said, "you'd ever wish to meet."

Each had his or her own compliment for someone that Jason immediately wished he could have met.

"Well, today is his birthday."

"How did he die?" Jason asked.

Hettie replied "Well, it was a brain tumour – took him very quickly and the doctors …"

"They let him down badly," said Emily, shaking her head in disgust.

Agnes agreed, "Yes, unforgivable … for three weeks they said it was just a bad headache."

"Anyway, he had one last wish," Clarrie said.

"That he should not be forgotten and that his life should forever light up our lives. So we do two things every year on his birthday," Jack added.

"Yes! Afternoon tea at the Penhelig Hotel," Hettie said.

"He adored afternoon tea," Maud explained.

"Sounds fantastic! And what's the other thing?" asked Jason.

"Ah, well I think you can help with that! Why don't we tell you over tea?" Agnes replied intriguingly.

So, later in the afternoon when all the chores had been done and the house was spic and span, they walked down the lane to the Penhelig Hotel and ordered afternoon tea.

Jason had never had an afternoon tea before and didn't realise that it involved copious cups of Darjeeling tea soaked up with plates and plates of very posh sandwiches, made with cheese, ham, cucumber, salmon, beef and so forth. These were brought out with teacakes, slices of Dundee cake and warm fruit scones, strawberry jam and clotted cream.

Of all the delicious things Jason would savour throughout the rest of his life this introduction, this first taste of scones, jam and cream would be the highlight.

Firstly Jack taught him how to spread the clotted cream thickly on the scone and then layer it with as much jam as possible, then … bite!

As the first mouthful hit his taste buds he realised he would be eating many more in the future and he gave an involuntary "Mmmyummmm" which made everyone laugh.

"I do believe he likes it!" Hettie said.

"Undoubtedly!" Maud replied smiling widely.

Finally, as they polished off the final fruitcake, the last course of the feast, they all raised their teacups in a toast.

"To Bill!" they all said, "To Bill!" came the reply.

Agnes said "Now there is one more thing but that needs to wait until it's dark."

"Yes, I checked," Jack said. "Eight would be perfect."

"What? What?" Jason asked.

"Oh you'll see Jason," Maud said, "and you'll be able to help."

They returned to Ty Angylion and Jason spent the afternoon trying to guess what the evening's secret operation would be and finally, after a very light evening meal given the excesses of afternoon tea, they gathered at the front door.

Each of the aunts wore a light wrap or scarf to protect them from the potential night chill. Hettie carried a small shopping bag with a flask and bottle in it.

Then Jack appeared followed by Clarrie, each carrying a old brown and battered box. One seemed fairly heavy and the other was a little shredded and rattled when you shook it.

They carried the boxes over to Penhelig Gardens and placed them by the bench.

Jason opened the first box, which appeared to be full of small tea lights – tiny candles - and a huge box of matches. The second box, the heavier, had a number of crossed bamboo sticks and a stack of what Jason thought were paper bags without handles.

"Whatever are they?" Jason asked scratching his head.

"They're sky lanterns! They'll light up the night!" Clarrie said.

"I'll show you," Jack said and took out a paper bag and a pair of sticks. He opened the base of the bag and inserted the pair of sticks like a cross to tension the bag and keep the end of it open. "All we need now is a candle," he said and placed a tea light on a nail which was situated at the point where the sticks crossed.

"Now, we light the little candle which creates the hot air. The hot air fills the bag and - hey presto - you have a hot air balloon – a sky lantern which you'll see for miles!" Jack said, very pleased with himself.

Agnes came over. "When father died he said that he hoped that his life had lit up the world for a short while. So Emily had a great idea of sending up lanterns every year on his birthday that would light up the world just for a short while."

"What a wonderful idea!" Jason said then thought for a moment, "How far will they go?"

Jack put a wet finger in the air, "Well I think..." and he pointed over the estuary, "...there's only a very light wind. They'll go towards Borth, Ynslas and then out to sea. Come on, let's do the first!"

Jack took the first lantern and carefully lit the candle, and with Jason and Clarrie supporting the top it began to fill with warm air. Within a few minutes Jason could feel the lantern just wanted to fly and after a nod from Clarrie they released it and watched as it soared slowly into the air where it was picked up by the light breeze.

Before they could enjoy it a second was already being prepared and soon another was skyward. The other sisters were now helping and another was released a minute or so later. Then another. And another.

"How many do you send?" Jason asked.

"Exactly forty-nine," Agnes said, "Bill's age when he died."

"How far will they go?" Jason asked quizzically.

"Perhaps 20 miles or so. It depends on the wind. The candle goes out and they'll fall gently into the sea," Jack replied.

Clarrie smiled, "I think some get to heaven you know."

Soon the box was looking decidedly empty and the last lantern was released into the air and it too found its way high into the indigo-blue night sky.

Jason, Jack and Clarrie walked to the wall and looked over the estuary. High over the river and into the distance beyond was a trail of candle-lit lanterns heading out towards the Irish Sea beyond.

It was one of the most incongruous and at the same time wonderful sights that Jack had ever seen and his eyes sparkled as he watched the lights fade into the darkness.

The aunts celebrated with a flask of hot tea and chocolate biscuits and for a few moments each was alone with their thoughts, remembering their father with fondness and love.

"A great man," Agnes said.

"Taken well before his time," Emily replied

"Too early," Clarrie added.

"A lovely man; a huge hug," Maud reflected.

"A huge hug," Hettie agreed.

"When did he die?" Jason asked.

"August 1920. Early in the evening at about this time," Jack said, his thoughts somewhere else, high in the night sky over Aberdovey.

Jason realised that Clarrie would only have been perhaps 11 or 12 and Emily perhaps in her late twenties when Bill died, but fifty years on he was still fondly remembered.

"I hope someone does that for me when I'm gone," Jason said quietly and Hettie who stood behind him hugged him from behind and he felt her comforting warmth on his back.

As the lights faded and the lanterns disappeared into the dark night there were sighs and they all began to gather their belongings and returned with the empty boxes back over the road.

"Until next year," Jack said.

"Yes. Next year," Clarrie agreed.

Wearily they crossed over the road for there was one final duty to perform; though the house was strictly speaking "chapel" which meant alcohol was never drunk, it had been agreed by Jack and his sisters that certain special occasions warranted a toast and their father's birthday was one such occasion.

The toast normally consisted of sherry with Jack taking a Glenfiddich whiskey and Maud prepared them dutifully. "Don't forget mine's a Cassis!" Clarrie said skipping through to the lounge.

"Jason you can come and help if you would," Maud said and he took a whiskey glass, and four sherry glasses from the glass cabinet.

"Five!" Maud corrected him; "I don't see why you shouldn't have a small tot in celebration."

She poured a measure of whiskey in Jack's cut-glass tumbler and a small measure of sherry into four glasses and placed both bottles on the tray. To this she added a bottle of Cassis.

She took out a bottle of blackcurrant cordial and poured it neat into Clarrie's glass. She smiled at Jason, "She just can't take alcohol, and both times she actually had alcohol she passed out. She thinks that this is Cassis," she said winking.

They carried the tray into the lounge where the glasses were handed out.

"Well, a toast to Bill Hughes!" Jack said and they each raised their glasses to their father.

The sisters, Jack and Jason sipped generously and Hettie and Jack both had another small glass.

"Clarrie, would you like another Cassis?" Maud asked smiling at Jason.

"Oh Maud, no; this is enough - I couldn't have another, I'd be tipsy!" Clarrie replied.

Jason smiled at the deception. "Do you remember that Bill's idea of a good bottle of wine was the percentage alcohol content," Jack said laughing, "the higher the number – the better the wine!"

"I remember buying some real paint stripper from a supermarket for his birthday dinner. He picked up the bottle, nodded his head and said 'Ah fourteen percent, very good!'"

At this the room filled with raucous laughter. Jason listened to the conversation and buzz in the room, and for a moment he felt as if he were one them. Included and at home.

13. Flight of an Angel

Psalm 91:11
*"For he will command his angels
to guard you in all your ways."*

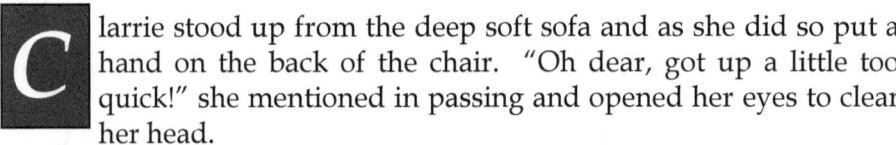larrie stood up from the deep soft sofa and as she did so put a hand on the back of the chair. "Oh dear, got up a little too quick!" she mentioned in passing and opened her eyes to clear her head.

"Are you okay?" Hettie asked, "You've gone quite pale."

"Oh, I'm fine. Just a little dizzy. I'll be okay in a moment." And taking a step she steadied herself again and smiled.

"I'll go out and sit on the front step and watch the boats on the estuary for a few minutes to get some air," she said and stretched.

"Good idea," Hettie said, "I'll get the tea on once I've finished this side of the quilt. I'll be half an hour."

"Well give me a call and I'll give you a hand when you're ready," Clarrie said and putting her hands on her hips turned to go and sighed deeply. "Honestly, I must be sleepy or getting old," she said yawning like a bear.

Hettie looked up nodded and smiled; "Oh don't Clarrie, you'll start me off!" and she stifled a yawn.

"I think I'll go and sit in the sunshine a while," Clarrie said. She slowed walked down the hall, took a cushion from the chest and then went through the open front door. A warm summer breeze blew up the stairs and aired the house. She threw the cushion onto the top step and sat down leaning against the railings.

She looked across the Dovey estuary towards Borth and the hills beyond and smiled. The little fishing boats bobbed on the calm water and the sun glistened on the water.

It warmed her aches and pains to the core and she sighed. "What a very beautiful day," she thought and thanked the Lord for her good fortune for living in such a peaceful place. Then gently closing her eyes she began to nap again.

Some hours later Jason came back up the Roman road with a lush bunch of pink and purple rhododendron flowers he'd picked for his aunts for the dining room table. He'd also found a knotted piece of driftwood for his uncle that he thought he could turn into a sculpture or some such. The sun warmed his back and as he walked he kicked the mussel shells dropped by the gulls in the grass in the park.

As he approached the house he saw Aunt Clarrie napping on the front step and called out but regretted it as soon as he had. Luckily he was too far away for her to hear and she did not respond. He felt stupid that he might have woken her and crossed the road to the side gate and let her continue her slumbers. He walked up the path and through the kitchen door. His Aunt Hettie was just turning on the gas to begin boiling the potatoes and he presented her with the flowers with his usual drama.

"Tah, dah!" he said. "Beautiful aren't they!"

"Oh, how lovely!" Hettie said, "Thank you! What beautiful rich colours." And reaching under the sink she pulled out a vase and filled it with water.

"There you go, pop them in there, I'll do them properly later and put them on the table. They'll make a fine centrepiece.

"I almost woke Clarrie on the front step as I came in. She's still fast asleep," Jason said.

"Never mind. I'll go and wake her. She'll get cranky if she sleeps too long. Why don't you lay the table for dinner?"

"Okey dokey!" Jason said and began sorting cutlery from the drawer.

Hettie walked from the kitchen and returned a few moments later, her face was lined with worry. "Jason, leave the cutlery a moment and fetch Agnes for me. She's in the back bedroom."

"What's wrong?" he asked.

"It's Clarrie. I can't seem to wake her. Hurry now," she said calmly but Jason could feel her consternation.

Jason scurried up the stairs and knocked on the bedroom door. Agnes was sorting out tea towels and blankets and clothes for the charity shop in the town.

"Aunt Agnes? Aunt Hettie says could you come quickly. Something's wrong with Clarrie."

Agnes left the pile on the bed and followed Jason who led the way. Hettie appeared from the kitchen.

"It's Clarrie. I tried to wake her but she's not stirring," Hettie said.

"Probably had one of her sleeping pills or some such." Agnes said trying to play down the concern in Hettie's voice.

Agnes went to the front step and knelt down and took Clarrie's hand. "Clarrie dear. Wake up. Its tea time almost," she said then she checked her pulse.

"Oh my Lord! Hettie fetch the blanket from the window seat. Jason I want you to run down to the big house behind the shop at Penhelig. Fetch Doctor Evans. Tell him to come quick. Run boy!" she said and in an instant he was on his way as fast as his legs could carry him. Hettie wrapped the blanket round Clarrie's shoulders and looked at Agnes. She bit her lip. It was the smallest of signs but Hettie knew what it meant.

Within minutes Doctor Evans arrived. His concern was immediately obvious. He felt Clarrie's pulse, touched her forehead, listened to her heart. Finally he took a small mirror from his bag to see if it misted. He shook his head; there was nothing he could do. She had passed.

Jason fetched his uncle and other aunts and Doctor Evans, helped by Jack, carried Clarrie into the lounge supporting her head with a pillow.

Through it all not a tear was shed or a word spoken. The sisters took it with a combined strength and stoicism.

"She just went to sleep," the Doctor said to Agnes as he left. "There was no pain. It was a brain aneurism."

A few hours later the undertakers arrived and took her away. Jason and Hettie couldn't watch and they sat in the dining room staring at each other across the table. Jason could see Hettie was filling with tears and reached out across the table and took her hand.

"I'm sorry," she said, "I loved my sister very much." Then after a few moments she added, "She was the youngest of us all. Only 61 years old. The youngest of us all." And with that she wept.

Jason let go her hand and stood up and went round and hugged her. "If me being here is a lot of trouble I'll go home?" he said.

Hettie looked at him and smiled through her tears, "By no means Jason! Clarrie would not have wanted such a thing."

"You're sure?" Jason questioned.

"Of course!" and Hettie uncharacteristically squeezed his arm.

Jason nodded, "Thank you!" and realised that in the few weeks he had been there he and his aunt Hettie had become closer and he hugged her.

"It will be alright," Jason said. It was something his mother always said when he was worried or concerned.

"I know," Hettie replied a tear trickling down her cheek.

14. Ascension

"What is there astonishing in the death of a mortal?
But we are grieved at his dying before his time.
Are we sure that this was not his time?
We do not know how to pick and choose what is good for our souls, or
how to fix the limits of the life of man."

Saint Basil the Great

During the few days after Clarrie's passing Jason's aunts and uncle spent much of their time arranging her funeral. The funeral was to be held a few days later on a Thursday. Many friends and relatives were invited and given the distance most would stay over either at "Ty Angylion" or with friends, in hotels or bed and breakfasts nearby.

At three on the Wednesday afternoon the undertakers arrived to lay Clarrie in her coffin in the front room "in sight of the window so she could have a last view of the bay," Emily had said.

Jason had never seen someone who was dead before, let alone in a coffin, and at first he was a little frightened. But, comforted and led by the hand by Emily and Jack, he was taken to "pay his last respects".

Clarrie looked asleep, at peace, almost as if she was going to wake up again. Emily kissed her on the forehead. Jack did the same and stroked Clarrie's greying hair and added with the weakest of smiles, "Good night sweetest princess, angels sing thee to thy rest."

Jack paused, lost for a moment in his grief, "Hamlet. Act 5. Scene..." his voice trailed off and he shook his head as if he couldn't remember or couldn't be bothered to add the scene number of the play.

With the light fading Emily switched on the table light in the window and closed the curtains. Turning towards the door she said, "Night, night Clarrie," and the three of them left the room and closed the door behind them.

Late on the Wednesday evening his mother and father arrived by car with cousins who Jason had never seen before. There had, he was told later, been the usual arguments about that fact that Jason's father should stay at the house rather than have to pay for accommodation, seeing he was the closest relative. Their arrival was therefore perfunctory rather than warm.

As they were late there was little time for conversation and after the briefest of greetings they all went to bed.

Hettie, Emily, Agnes, Maud and Jack were up at 6:00 am the next morning for there was still much to do. Jason joined them a little after 6:30 am and set about buttering bread and helping Agnes and Maud make piles of sandwiches and cutting slices of cake for the guests that would come back to the house after the funeral.

For a few hours grief was forgotten as the focus was on the task of preparing for guests later in the day. Clarrie was at the centre of the conversation and specifically her infectious sense of humour.

Jason's parents and cousins appeared at around 9:00 am with a clear expectation of being provided with a full English breakfast and, this not being forthcoming, they reluctantly settled for tea and toast made by Jack.

At around 10:30 am everyone retired to his or her room to get ready and Jason was handed a thin black tie and grey jacket by his mother. "Wear your school trousers with it," she added.

While he dressed he heard the chapel bell at the other end of the town tolling dolefully in the distance.

He went down the stairs to see the coffin being carried by the undertakers to the hearse parked outside the house.

"Which car shall we go in?" his mother asked Hettie.

"Car? Oh, I see. No, we're walking to the chapel," Hettie replied much to his mother's surprise.

"Oh well, I see, I'm sure we'll..." she stammered looking at Jason's father for some support.

The traffic had been stopped and Jason was surprised to see the streets lined with friends and neighbours carrying flowers and dressed in black as a mark of respect.

The hearse pulled away and drove off at a few miles an hour. Immediately behind it were Jack, Hettie and Emily and behind them Agnes and Maud. Agnes winked at Jason that he should come with them and he went to stand between them. Jason's parents, cousins and other relatives were behind them.

The hearse went under the Penhelig railway bridge and turned the corner past the shop and Jason looked behind him to see villagers join the back of the procession.

He heard Hettie and Emily occasionally sob and could tell Maud and Agnes was also holding back their tears.

Jason noted that every shop was closed and seemingly every window had their blinds drawn as a mark of respect.

As they passed the mussel beds Maud turned to Jason and said, "I remember her when she was a little younger than you splashing around there. She got us a tanning once for soaking our Sunday dresses. She was always the mischievous one!" and she smiled.

The procession then became silent as they passed street upon street of mourners, who bowed their heads and removed their hats as the hearse went past.

As they left the town the sky began to cloud over and what had been a sunny day turned grim and the sky became a dour, leadened, gunmetal grey. By the time they reached the chapel with the Reverend standing at the cemetery gates Jason realised that the whole of the village had followed the hearse from Angel House to the cemetery on the north side of the town. The coffin was carried gently into the small chapel and the chapel doors left open so that the many that could not get inside could join in the service.

Carrie's favourite hymns "All Things Bright and Beautiful" and "Abide with Me" were sung. It was a hymn that Jason had never heard before but though it was heartfelt and tuneful it was a hymn he could not listen to without a lump coming to his throat from then on.

Finally Jack said a few words. At the end he struggled to say his final eulogy: "She was my sister and I will miss her with all my heart. When I close my eyes I will forever see her smile and when I open them I will forever see her smile in the sunniest of days dancing on the waters of the estuary."

Then with shaking hands Agnes stood and read a poem which Clarrie had loved:

It Was an English Ladye Bright

It was an English ladye bright,
(The sun shines fair on Carlisle wall,)
And she would marry a Scottish knight,
For Love will still be lord of all.

Blithely they saw the rising sun
When he shone fair on Carlisle wall;
But they were sad ere day was done,
Though Love was still the lord of all.

Her sire gave brooch and jewel fine,
Where the sun shines fair on Carlisle wall;
Her brother gave but a flask of wine,
For ire that Love was lord of all.

For she had lands both meadow and lea,
Where the sun shines fair on Carlisle wall,
And he swore her death, ere he would see
A Scottish knight the lord of all.

That wine she had not tasted well
(The sun shines fair on Carlisle wall,)
When dead, in her true love's arms, she fell,
For Love was still the lord of all!

He pierced her brother to the heart,
Where the sun shines fair on Carlisle wall:--
So perish all would true love part
That Love may still be lord of all!

And then he took the cross divine,
Where the sun shines fair on Carlisle wall,
And died for her sake in Palestine;
So Love was still the lord of all.

Now all ye lovers, that faithful prove,
(The sun shines fair on Carlisle wall,)
Pray for their souls who died for love,
For Love shall still be lord of all!

She finished by repeating the final line, "For love shall still be Lord of all!" as if it were a credo.

And even though Jack had witnessed death, sorrow and carnage in his life tears began to trickle gently down his cheek.

Then the coffin was carried quietly to the cemetery.

Jason laid a fresh bunch of rhododendrons on the casket and stood by Hettie's side and squeezed her hand. She smiled with thanks and laid a bunch of wild flowers she'd picked from the kitchen garden.

As they began to walk from the grave the bible-black sky that had threatened to open did so and a light Welsh mountain rain began to fall.

Jason was handed a huge black umbrella and he held it over each of his aunts as they said goodbye to their sister at the graveside and walked back to the road.

As they walked back to Angel House in silence the rain became heavy, the thick drenching rain that rolls off the Welsh mountains black, grim and doom-laden.

Not before time they arrived back at the house and began handing out the plates of sandwiches and slices of fruitcake. It seemed to Jason that everyone from the village went back to the house for sandwiches and tea and Jason helped hand out plates and take people's coats.

Late in the afternoon only his aunts, uncle and close family were left. As the afternoon wore on the rain eased, then stopped and he and his father crossed the street to the park gardens.

"I remember many a picnic on these lawns," his father said. "Can you remember when I took you out in the little boat onto the river?" he asked.

"No? Jason said, "When was that?"

"Oh, it was the summer I had our first car. 1959. I think perhaps 1960," his father replied.

Jason smiled, "I would have been one or two Dad," he said matter-of-factly.

"Ah, perhaps you wouldn't have remembered then," his father replied.

There was a pregnant silence and then his father said, "We're trying Jason."

Jason looked at his father who was staring at the ground with his hands in his pockets. It was obvious that the conversation had been terminated.

With their focus on the many relatives at the funeral his parents hardly spoke to him throughout the rest of the day.

Finally the time approached for their drive back to the Midlands. His father and mother took him to one side.

"We suggested you come back with us Jason," his father said. "I thought you'd been annoying them or getting in the way," and he shrugged dismissively.

"But your aunts wouldn't hear of it," his mother replied smiling.

"Be a good boy now Jason," his father said and his mother kissed his cheek, whispered "I love you" in his ear and got into the car with his dad.

Jason trudged back into the house and looked at the clock. It was almost a quarter to eight and frankly he felt worn out. Jack was standing in the bay window as if in a daze lost in his thoughts as he watched the lights of Borth twinkle into life.

"I'm off to bed now Uncle Jack," Jason said.

There was no reply. "Uncle Jack?" he said again.

Jack snapped from his thoughts, "Mmm? Yes?"

"Just off to bed," Jason repeated.

"Oh. Yes of course," Jack said.

Jason looked at him a little closer for a second. His face was flushed and his eyes were red and bloodshot. Jason thought that he had perhaps been crying.

"Are you okay Uncle Jack?" he probed. "Would you like me to sit and chat with you a while?"

"No, No. I'm fine," Jack replied, lying very badly, "just a little worn out by the day. You go on up. I'll be on my way myself in a trice!" and he attempted to lift his voice at the end of the sentence to lighten his sadness. Jason smiled and realised Jack wanted to be left alone with his thoughts.

"Good night then," Jason said and began to wearily climb the stairs to bed.

"Yes. Good night," and then under his breath Jack said, "Good night Clarrie. Sleep well my darling little sister. I love you." And the tears once more welled from his eyes and trickled in rivers onto his jacket.

But by then Jason was already out of earshot.

15. Charity

No one leaves you
When you live in their heart and mind
And no one dies
They just move to the other side
When we're gone
Watch the world simply carry on
It's okay, we will stay and be happy
Stay and be happy
With those who have loved us today

Steve Hogarth

The day following the funeral Maud and Hettie were in a bustle and Jason believed it was their way to cover their grief and emotions.

Maud had decided to rise early and had already begun to clear Clarrie's wardrobes out to give any clothes which weren't too old or worn out to the Red Cross shop in the Main Street.

Jason was asked if he would clear out the drawers in the dressing table and put anything useable in a box to go through later and anything that was rubbish into a black plastic bin bag.

In one of the drawers Jason found a book of poetry with some of the pages marked. Many were romantic poems by Browning, Yeats, Shelley and Christina Rossetti and he realised it gave him a slightly different view of Clarrie; she was a romantic at heart, yearning to be loved and adored.

He opened the book at the last poem, one by Charles Dickens:

Things that Never Die

Things that never die.
The pure, the bright,
The beautiful that stirred our hearts in youth,
The impulses to wordless prayer,
The streams of love and truth,
The longing after something lost,
The spirit's yearning cry,
The striving after better hopes
These things can never die.
The timid hand stretched forth to aid
A brother in his need;
A kindly word in grief's dark hour
That proves a friend indeed;
The plea for mercy softly breathed,
When justice threatens high,
The sorrow of a contrite heart
These things shall never die.
Let nothing pass, for every hand
Must find some work to do,
Lose not a chance to waken love
Be firm and just and true.
So shall a light that cannot fade
Beam on thee from on high,
And angel voices say to thee –
"These things shall never die."

As Jason read, Maud had sat down on the bed and watched him as he scanned the poem. "I remember her reading that at our father's funeral," she said, "poor girl cried for days after."

Jason could see his Aunt Maud getting a little emotional and he hugged her.

"Oh, I'm just being silly. Just very silly," she said wiping a tear from her cheek.

"No, it's right to cry for those who have gone," Jason said.

"You're right – such an old head on young shoulders," Maud said, "but she's not gone of course. I can hear her voice in my head any time."

"I'll miss her. She was a lot of fun!" Jason said.

100

"Yes. Perhaps a lesson for me there!" Maud said nudging Jason playfully.

Jason helped Maud carry the boxes to the cellar and stack them.

"I'll get Mr Price to pick them up later," Maud said then, thinking, she added, "Would you like to walk into town with me? I need to get a few things. We're out of milk and low on bread. We could maybe get a cup of tea and a cake at the café."

Jason nodded. This was not normal behaviour for Aunt Maud but he realised that at this moment, this morning, she needed company and young company at that.

As they walked along the High Street Maud commented that the cottage opposite the mussel beds, 'Bryn Helig', had been sold and wondered whom it might have been sold to.

"I hope they're a nice couple and join in at the chapel. The more the merrier!" she said.

"Perhaps it's not a couple?" Jason queried.

"Perhaps," Maud said absentmindedly and she continued at a brisk pace into the town.

Her errands were few; she posted a couple of letters at the post office, bought a packet of Earl Grey tea and some Battenberg cake from the supermarket, and popped into the Red Cross shop to ask them to pick up Clarrie's clothes "at their convenience". Finally she bought a Woman's Realm for herself and a Melody Maker paper for Jason from the corner shop.

Within half an hour she was done and they were sitting in the Red Dragon Tea Shop; Maud sipping a hot cup of tea and Jason slurping on a Coke while they shared a buttered toasted teacake.

"Actually it's rather nice to get out; I think I get stuck in that kitchen far too much!" Maud said uncharacteristically.

"Well you do seem to do all the cooking," Jason said.

"Yes, maybe we could have a rota," Maud replied then she smiled. "Mind you there would only be Hettie and I on it. Jack can only cook eggs and bacon, Emily's sight is going and Agnes hates cooking."

"You could make it simpler; perhaps cook in batches and keep it in the freezer. Like your boil-in-the-bag breakfasts," Jason said.

101

"Mmmm, what a good idea. Might mean I spend less time overall in the kitchen," she said and finished her tea. "Come on. We'll have a choc ice on the way home."

Now this was very out of character for Maud but Jason thought it about time for all that.

They popped back into the paper shop and Maud paid for a choc ice for herself and a Fab ice lolly for Jason as usually when he ate choc ice most of it found its way onto his t-shirt.

By the time they were back at the cottage the ice creams were finished and Maud was still contemplating who had moved in.

"It could be a young couple I suppose." Then she reconsidered, "But what would they do around here? If there'd been any jobs the gossip would have got around by now."

As they walked up the steps Jason saw Maud quickly glancing at the step where Clarrie has passed. He thought he might take her mind off it and thanked her for the trip out.

"You're welcome young man. Always pleased to have the company," Maud said sighing and took her magazine into the lounge. As she sat down she slapped the magazine on the back of the sofa and said to herself "You know, perhaps I could take up knitting again!"

But Jason was now out of earshot; it was time for him to read his own magazine.

As he read he found himself drifting off to sleep on the bed; he woke and hour later to again hear the faint sound of sobbing.

He strained to hear where it was coming from and put an ear to the wall adjoining the next room but couldn't hear anything. It was very faint and he decided it must have originated from downstairs.

He sighed; it was certainly a mystery, he'd heard it a couple of times before and at night. He resolved to ask Aunt Maud when he went downstairs. But for now the sound had ceased and he was happy staring at the ceiling and just kicking his heels on the bed.

16. Brothers in Arms

Revelation 12: 7-8
*7 Then war broke out in heaven.
Michael and his angels fought against the dragon,
and the dragon and his angels fought back.
8 But he was not strong enough,
and they lost their place in heaven.*

*J*ason sat on the bed and thought more about the crying he had heard earlier in the afternoon. It was the same as he sometimes heard during the night and was more of a cry of anguish than one of grief. Was it one of the aunts grieving over Clarrie? Was it a baby next door perhaps? Perhaps it was a ghost? He decided that once and for all he would find out and descended the stairs to the kitchen where he found Maud peeling potatoes for lunch.

"Aunt Maud?" Jason asked.

"Mmm, Jason," Maud replied absentmindedly.

"I keep hearing crying, sobbing some nights?" He shrugged, "Do you have any idea who or what it could be?"

"Oh yes," Maud said sadly and dropped the peeler and potato and dried her hands on a kitchen towel.

"I'm sure he won't mind me telling you," she said. "It's your Uncle Jack. Clarrie's passing has made him a little worse you know. Jack served in the First War and was eventually invalided out. He suffers from a type of shell shock. He saw awful, terrible things."

"Would it help him to talk about them?" Jason asked.

"Oh, he's spoken about them many times, "Maud replied, "but those sort of memories don't fade with time. They're etched onto your consciousness like a painting."

"Do you know where he is?" Jason asked.

"He's over in the park with his pipe and tobacco," Maud replied. "Why don't you go and sit with him for a while?"

Jason walked over to the park from the house and found Jack sitting on the bench, smoking his pipe, wisps of cherry smoke floated on the breeze. Jack was staring across the estuary in contemplation. His eyes seemed to be full of tears.

"I'm sorry Jason," Jack said, "It's been many a year but the things I have seen are not those that can be washed clean, even with time."

"Was this the war?" Jason asked.

"Yes. First World War, 1914 to 1918. In history the greatest waste of human life that there has been. Criminal."

"How old were you?"

"I wasn't more than three years older than you are now Jason, when I went off to war. 1915. Four of us - James Eldon, Tom Matthews, Alistair Freeman and I – we were all at Oxford studying. We all joined up together. I remember my mother was heartbroken. My Dad gave me a good leathering. I don't blame them though. I'd have done the same but we just wanted to make a difference. You see, didn't take us long to work out it was a bloody waste of time."

"After basic training I was posted to Ypres in November 1914, and I saw my regiment drop one-by-one, day after day. Saw James and Alistair cut to pieces by machine guns. James got caught on the wire and Alistair tried to help him out. No use of course. We had to recover the bodies after dark."

"As the months went on I could see Tom beginning to become more and more remote. When I spoke to him he would smile and say, 'It's OK Jack. I've got a plan to get out.' I thought it was some crazy scheme to feign sickness or something."

"Well, one day we were waiting to go over the top. By then I was corporal. Last man standing and all that. Suddenly the order comes: 'Wait ten minutes for the flare!'"

"When we see the flare, off we go! Suddenly Tom says 'Don't worry mates I speak some German, I'll go and have a word with them!' We tried to grab him but he was already halfway up the ladder. And with that he climbs up the ladder, drops his gun and begins to wave towards the German lines as if he had spotted some old friends on the beach at Brighton. We're shouting and yelling for him to get down and then 'Bang!' A single shot from a sniper. Dropped like a tree into the mud. Bullet took him right between the eyes. I'll never forget his face. Surprise. The look of shock and surprise on his face! He really believed he could stop the carnage."

Jack drew on pipe and inhaled, nursing the bowl between his shaking hand. Jon could not tell whether it was through grief, fear or anger.

"Not long after I got promoted to sergeant. Posted to this new-fangled invention, the tank," Jack shrugged, "bloody death traps."

"I ended up commanding one of them. Four of us inside. Me and three others, driver and gunners. Driver was from the next village – bloke called Bill Unwin. First day we took off and raced across a field towards what we think is lightly defended German lines. Turns out there's a bloody big gun in the middle of it. Shell fire and bang a direct hit on the front of the tank. Explosion takes off the head of the driver and kills the other two, leaving me bruised but alive. I manage to crawl out of the wreck back to the medics. I arrive an hour later covered head-to-toe in so much blood the doc says that he thinks I'm badly injured."

"He starts to patch me up and gives me a towel to wipe my face. I do so and look down and stare at a towel smeared with the brains of my mate Bill. I pass out on the floor. Next thing I remember I'm in a hospital somewhere in Surrey."

"Don't believe what they tell you, what you hear, what the politicians and the war-mongers say. Once more into the breech indeed! Damn their eyes."

"War is not glorious. It is not. It stinks. It's terrible. Awful. Horrible. Nearly sixty years on, there is not a day goes by when I don't hear the guns, smell the death, see the broken bodies, feel the warmth of my friend's blood on my face."

Then Jack fell silent. He slumped on the bench as if exhausted. He didn't sob but Jason saw a single tear trickle gently down his cheek.

"Is that the crying I can hear some nights?" he asked.

Jack smiled. "Yes, my boy. Sometimes I can't sleep with those thoughts and releasing them is a good way of getting me off to sleep."

"I can imagine seeing your friends die makes you very hard. Cynical even?" Jason asked.

"Yes, exactly," Jack said. "That's why I worked in pharmaceuticals for forty years. Helping to cure disease, not taking life. Someone once said that war is sometimes a necessary evil. Well, no matter how necessary, it is always an evil." There was anger in Jack's eyes now.

"Since then I suffer the most horrendous nightmares – wake in the night sixty years on screaming in pain. Can you imagine that?" Jason shook his head, how could he imagine those sorts of images etched onto one's memory.

Then Jack said, "I'm sorry I told you my story but..." then he thought for a moment. "Have you ever heard of Mahatma Ghandi?"

"Yes, I have. I saw his picture in the newspaper once," Jason said.

"Well, he was a great man. A peaceful man. Another taken by a bullet. He said, 'If we are to teach real peace in this world, and if we are to carry on a real war against war, we shall have to begin with the children.'"

"Then I shall become part of the real war against war," Jason said paraphrasing Ghandi's words.

"Come on," Jack stood up smiling, his gloomy spirits lifted. "Let's see if Maud has any Dorset Apple Cake left!" he said, changing the mood.

"And a cup of tea," Jason added.

"Oh yes, tea and cake. You just can't have the one wi'owt t'other!" Jack said slapping his knees, now smiling broadly. And with this they returned to the house.

17. Change and Time

"The purpose of religion is
not to build beautiful churches or temples,
but to cultivate positive human qualities
such as tolerance, generosity and love."

The Dalai Lama

One morning Jason was asked to pop to the little Penhelig Store down the street as Maud was out of lard to cook the breakfast batch of bacon, egg and sausages. The morning was a little cold and his walk was brisk on the way there.

There was a chill wind off the sea and he put his hands in his pockets to keep them warm. On the way back to Angel House he looked along the main road and something out of the ordinary caught his eye.

Outside the little sea-front cottage, which they had noticed before had been sold; a large Pickford's removal lorry was parked. It must have arrived very early in the morning. The tailgate was open and men in brown coats and overalls were moving in furniture through the front door.

Jason saw the removal men carry in a couple of chairs, a writing desk, a table lamp and a plant. Then one of the men saw him standing in the middle of the street, stopped and waved to show he'd been spotted being nosey. He instantly felt embarrassed by his curiosity but instinctively waved back anyway. The man laughed.

Arriving back at the house Jason told the others what he considered was hot news. "Bryn Helig is being moved into!" he announced to anyone caring to listen and wanting to know.

"What, the cottage?" Hettie asked.

"Yes, the one on the seafront opposite the mussel beds and shingle beach. They'll have a very good view out of their lounge windows," he replied.

"Did you see who it was? Did they look a nice couple?" Maud asked.

"No. I only saw the removal men," Jason said, and then thought for a moment. "Do you want me to go and find out?" he added in a rash of overconfidence.

"Absolutely not!" Maud said, "If they are good neighbours they will introduce themselves in the next few days or in chapel if they are good church goers, which I trust they are!"

The possibility that they might not be or even might not be a couple had not entered Maud's consciousness so the subject was dropped and the important business of cooking the usual hearty breakfast for a house full was begun.

Over breakfast the aunts and Jack were in especially reflective mood.

"So, if you don't mind me asking, when was each of you born?" Jason asked. "And what happened in the year you were born?" he added.

"Well," Emily said, "I was born in 1891, that was the year that, well I'm not sure?"

Agnes interjected, "Sergei Prokofiev was born."

"And the first penalty was awarded in English football for Wolverhampton Wanderers!" Jack said and there was general laugher at this piece of trivia.

"Well it was!" Jack said.

"I was born in 1893," Agnes piped up, "I was told they discovered gold in Australia; Dvorak performed his New World Symphony for the first time and Conan Doyle published the 'Final Problem', killing off Sherlock Holmes."

"Very auspicious!" Maud said.

"Clarrie was born in 1912. She was such a cute baby," Agnes said, "can't remember anything that happened in 1912."

"Titanic sank in April 1912," Jack said, "I remember I was Jason's age and I kept all the cuttings. I was born in 1898."

"Well, I was born in 1896, the only one not born in Aberdovey. Mum had to be taken to Aberystwyth as I was a breech birth," Maud said, "Oh, and I was told in 1896 they had the Olympics in Athens, Queen Victoria became the longest serving monarch, oh and Ira Gershwin was born – I love Gershwin!" then she prompted Hettie.

"Ah of course, just at the turn of the century in 1901, the year Queen Victoria died and King Edward VII came to the throne," Hettie said.

"Oh, I didn't like him!" Agnes said, "Pompous layabout!" she added.

"And what did you do in the war?" Jason asked inquisitively.

"Which one?" and they all laughed.

"Both!" Jason said.

"Well Jack volunteered in the First of course – he was only 16," Agnes said and Jack smiled remembering the day he signed up at the Town Hall in Aberdovey. Emily and I had had some basic medical training and were nurses in the field hospitals in France," Agnes added.

"Maud, Hettie and little Clarrie were too young to do anything in the first," Jack said, "but you worked at Bletchley Park with the code breakers in the Second, didn't you Hettie?"

"Oh yes, very hush, hush," Hettie said, "Clarrie fell in love with that soldier I introduced her to, remember?"

"Yes, poor soul. Survived the war unscathed and was killed in a car accident in London in October 1945," Hettie said.

There was a moment's reflection. "Do you think they'd have married?" Jason asked.

"Who knows?" Maud said, "Perhaps."

"He was a charming young man," Hettie said with a heavy sigh.

"We are getting a little down, aren't we?" Jack said and then took a deep breath, "Well, I think I should tell you about all my girlfriends!"

"Oh no!" Maud said, "Not in front of Jason. He's very impressionable!"

"Well there was this girl I met…" he started.

"No Jack! Absolutely not!" Hettie said, "Some of your stories. Honestly. Go and make yourself useful and make another pot of tea."

Jack winked at Jason, "One afternoon. When we're away from the ladies."

And suitably chastised Jack went to the kitchen and put the kettle on.

18. Rekindling a Flame

We can't cross a bridge until we come to it;
but I always like to lay down a pontoon ahead of time.

I t is strange how that summer surprises seemed to appear from nowhere. Just when everyone was in harmony and rhythm an event occurred which no one was expecting; least of all the aunts.

It was about ten on a Saturday morning and Jason was helping clear the dining room table. He saw an elderly gentleman, perhaps in his early seventies, walking up the main road from the direction of the town. He held a leather-bound book in his hand and occasionally looked into the cloudless blue sky and smiled. He seemed to be confident and enjoying the beautiful morning.

At first Jason ignored him and expected he was on his way to walk through the park and along the estuary, perhaps a tourist, but as he came to the railings outside Angel House he walked purposefully up the stone steps, to the front door and rang the bell. Twice.

Jason was about to answer it but Hettie had arrived at the door first and opened it.

There was a gasp and then she said excitedly, "Oh my goodness! What a surprise!"

"A pleasant one I do hope!" the man replied.

"Yes! Yes! Of course! Come on in, come on in!" she said a little flustered.

"Is she in?" the man asked. Hettie replied "Of course – goodness of course!" then she turned to Jason who'd been standing in the dining room doorway. "Jason please take Robert to the lounge. I'll go and fetch her."

Robert offered Jason a hand and Jason shook it. "Pleased to meet you Jason," the man said.

111

"Likewise. Please, come through and take a seat. The sofa has a good view of the sea," Jason said politely.

He could hear a commotion of excitement upstairs and then Agnes appeared at the lounge door.

"Mrs Agnes Ellis!" Robert said grandly.

"Mr Robert Hawthorne!" Agnes replied and she kissed him on the cheek in a way that showed some past and perhaps deep tenderness between them. She sat down on one of the easy chairs with Robert next to her on the sofa.

Then Hettie, Maud and Emily all appeared and there was a great exchange of greetings and they all agreed that it must have been 50 years since they had seen Robert last.

"Well not quite, perhaps 45!" he laughed.

Robert was quite a tall man; Jason had noted that even given his age he did not stoop. He was bright and alert and seemingly intelligent with a quick wit and good sense of humour.

Jason considered Robert well educated and that he probably had done some military service. He was smartly dressed in light trousers and wore a blue shirt, smart striped tie and dark blue double-breasted casual jacket.

The room was lit up with conversation and memories of long ago being exchanged as if they had happened only yesterday. Jason was content and listened intently to the exchange.

"And your husband Agnes?" Robert asked and Jason realised that of all the aunts Agnes would have been the one who had been married and he had never thought to ask.

"James died ten years ago now," she said, a hint of sadness in her voice, "he was a little older than us of course," she added.

"I'm very sorry to hear it, my condolences," Robert said.

"Well it was a while ago," Agnes said then added, "our saddest news is poor Clarrie. She passed just a few weeks ago."

"Oh, that is sad news. I think she was a teenager the last I saw her." Robert shook his head, "And what about Jack. Please don't tell me..."

At which moment Jack burst into the room and Jason suspected he had waited for a grand entrance.

"Absolutely not Hawthorne!" Jack said and at once Robert and he were shaking hands and hugging like old friends.

"But what brings you out to Wales and Aberdovey, Robert?" Maud asked inquisitively.

"I've bought 'Bryn Helig' in the main street!" Robert said to cries of 'Wonderful!' and 'Fantastic!' "When Charlotte died I came back from Germany; nothing to keep me there and I decided I wanted to end my days here."

"Well I never!" Maud said, "I was convinced a couple of old crocks had bought it as a holiday home."

"Whereas one old crock has bought it as his permanent home!" and there was general laughter.

Tea, cake, biscuits and memories were shared and exchanged.

It became evident that Jack and Robert had been university chums at Cambridge and had studied and indeed acted together, at which point Jack pointed to Jason, nodded and said, "My protégé – a young talent."

Robert has served in the Medical Corp when he met Agnes and it seemed to Jason they had been what was called 'an item'. Somehow there had been an amicable parting of the ways. Agnes had married James Ellis and Robert had married a German girl called Charlotte. They had lived in South Germany for many years, had had a son and a daughter both now living in Australia. Charlotte had died three years previously and with no real family left in Germany Robert had returned to the UK and for a few years lectured at Edinburgh University.

"Do you still write?" Jack asked.

"Oh, yes. The occasional magazine article and novel, which my agent tells me sells well. I write under a pseudonym. The royalty cheques help pay for a few little luxuries of course." Then absentmindedly he looked at his watch.

"I shouldn't keep you, I should..." he said, but Maud interjected.

"Nonsense! We haven't seen you for heaven knows how many years. You'll stay for lunch and we'll have no argument."

"Well if you insist..." Robert said.

"We do!" and there was a chorus of agreement.

"The more the merrier!" Jack said.

"Perhaps we should open some wine?" Agnes ventured.

"I think I can help there!" Robert said, "I brought a case of German Baden Weissherbst wine with me to the house. I'll pop back and get a couple! Maybe more!"

From that day on for the rest of Jason's stay the aunts and Jack made regular trips to Bryn Helig with Robert visiting pretty much every other day for lunch or dinner.

During the period Jason saw a marked change not only in Jack, who seemed to become less intense, but most of all in Agnes, who seemed to have had a great weight lifted from her shoulders as if she had finally managed to accept the loss of first her husband and then her beloved sister. There was a spring in her step and blush in her cheeks that bloomed whenever Robert was around and it seemed to warm not just Agnes, but all those in Ty Angylion.

19. The Gift

Revelations 5: 11-12
Then I looked and heard the voice of many angels,
numbering thousands upon thousands,
and ten thousand times ten thousand.

O ne morning Jack patted Jason on the back. "Well young man, a few days until your Mum and Dad pick you up and take you away from us. And I think it's time to go for the big one."

"The big one?" Jason asked shrugging his shoulders.

"The big speech. The zenith of Shakespearean prose, unrivalled in the English literature. Hamlet – the speech." And he took from his jacket pocket two old copies of Hamlet. One was dated 1936, Wolverhampton Grammar School Form I-A, the other simply said 'To Jack, Love Mum and Dad X, 1906'.

Jack took Jason's copy and opened it at the appropriate page and handed it to him.

"Now. We find Hamlet questioning his own mortality. He has a father murdered, been betrayed by his mother and girlfriend. His best friends have deserted him – he wonders whether to live or die." He took a deep breath. "Now centre, imagine you are in his situation – find a similar experience to lock onto."

And taking a few moments and locking onto the memory of seeing his aunt lying at rest in the front room some weeks before Jason began the speech:

> *To be, or not to be: that is the question:*
> *Whether 'tis nobler in the mind to suffer*
> *The slings and arrows of outrageous fortune,*
> *Or to take arms against a sea of troubles,*
> *And by opposing end them? To die: to sleep;*
> *No more; and by a sleep to say we end*

The heart-ache and the thousand natural shocks
That flesh is heir to, 'tis a consummation
Devoutly to be wish'd. To die, to sleep;
To sleep: perchance to dream:

Then Jack interjected "Think what would it be like to be asleep, forever, in oblivion?"

.....ay, there's the rub;
For in that sleep of death what dreams may come
When we have shuffled off this mortal coil,
Must give us pause: there's the respect
That makes calamity of so long life;
For who would bear the whips and scorns of time,
The oppressor's wrong, the proud man's contumely,
The pangs of despised love, the law's delay,
The insolence of office and the spurns
That patient merit of the unworthy takes,
When he himself might his quietus make
With a bare bodkin? who would fardels bear,
To grunt and sweat under a weary life,
But that the dread of something after death,
The undiscover'd country from whose bourn
No traveller returns, puzzles the will
And makes us rather bear those ills we have
Than fly to others that we know not of?

"So should Hamlet send his uncle, a murderer, killer of his father to that world?"

Thus conscience does make cowards of us all;
And thus the native hue of resolution
Is sicklied o'er with the pale cast of thought,
And enterprises of great pith and moment
With this regard their currents turn awry,
And lose the name of action.

Jack slapped his knees, clapped his hands and exclaimed "Brilliant!"

Jason hadn't realised that throughout the speech Agnes, Emily, Hettie and Maud had been standing behind him listening. They broke into applause, "Bravo, Jason! Bravo," they clapped, "Bravo!"

Then, much out of character and to Jason's surprise, Maud reached out and hugged him, "You've come a long way young man. We're all very proud of you."

Jason looked up and saw Maud's eyes filling with tears and she dabbed them with her hanky. "Oh, how silly and immature," she said scolding herself.

"Well done Jason," Agnes said, "you have a great talent." And he was hugged by each of his aunts in turn.

Jason looked down and noticed Agnes was now wearing a large ruby ring on her wedding ring finger. She smiled, "Robert asked that I should wear it." And Jason could see a hint of happiness and deep feelings for someone special in her cornflower-blue eyes.

"And! We have another gift for you," Hettie said. "We think as the youngest of our family it is right to pass on our family history such that it can nurtured as we have nurtured it." And from behind the sofa she picked up the thick brown family album and handed it to Jason.

"One of the last things Clarrie had made was a quilted bag for it to protect the cover," Emily said, "I've finished it for her." And she placed the album with great ceremony in the bag.

"Remember, love and family are your most precious gifts. They are freely given and freely accepted. They are the most valuable gifts anyone can give to you," Hettie said and kissed his forehead tenderly.

"And now we should have tea and cake!" Jack said. For one of the final times in the holiday they gathered as a family and shared their time, their laughter, their hopes and dreams and the minutiae that turn those times of our life into precious memories.

20. Tilling the Earth

Corinthians 3

7 So then neither the one who plants nor the one who waters is anything, but God who causes the growth.
8 Now he who plants and he who waters are one; but each will receive his own reward according to his own labour.
9 For we are God's fellow workers; you are God's field, God's building.

One Thursday afternoon Jason was summoned to the kitchen by Maud who seemed to be having an argument with Jack and which at first Jason thought he was the cause of.

"Well it's your own fault," Maud said, "I've told you not to sleep on the floor. It's silly at your age."

"Well I like sleeping on the floor. It feels...," and Jack searched for the right word, "more... comfortable."

Even Jason didn't think it sounded too convincing.

"Well I needed someone to pull some carrots and potatoes from the kitchen garden for me. If it wasn't for Jason they would go rotten," Maud said labouring the point.

"Well I'm sorry. I'll sleep on the bed next time," Jack said and turned to Jason. "Come on young man, there's far too much nagging going on here for my liking." Maud tutted in disgust.

"We need to pull up some carrots, perhaps some leeks – they're ready, and dig a few potatoes. We need some tools!" Jack said walking along the path up to the shed and opening the door.

Jason looked inside. Every tool looked oiled and pristine even though you could tell that they were old. Each was hung on its own hook with a label next to it.

"A good workman looks after his tools," Jack said grabbing a hoe and fork. "You look after them and they'll look after you."

Over the period of an hour they had dug up all the carrots, some of which looked a little damaged. "Still edible though," Jack said.

They moved on with Jason doing the digging and Jack supervising. Jack tried to make light of the work.

"Look! Jason stands in the potatoes and leeks!" he said and Jason laughed.

"Just be glad Maud isn't standing in the cabbages and peas!" Jason replied.

"Oh yes! Very good!" Jack said holding his side and then winced.

"Owww. Did my back in; bit stiff and I can't bend. I couldn't go to the disco anymore!" he said wiggling his hips, which made Jason laugh.

Soon they had a bucket full of potatoes and had pulled a dozen huge leeks. They then moved over to the garden tap where they rinsed what was left of the soil, which hadn't come off when they pulled them up.

Jason looked up and could see wide-eyed and bushy-tailed Briar the cat watching them as they worked. He absentmindedly washed a paw and then yawned.

Jack offered Briar the top of a carrot, which Briar swiped at with his paw and then in disgust jumped off the wall onto the rail-track side.

"Crazy mog!!" Jack said.

Hettie appeared with a battered round metal tray with two mugs of tea and some chocolate biscuits.

"For the workers!" she said and sitting on an old metal bench, which had certainly seen better days, they took a break.

"You must have seen some things in your life which are crazy; unexplainable," Jason said.

"Some pretty awful things too as you know Jason" Jack said, "There is one incident that springs to mind as unexplainable, like those strange FOU things in the sky."

"You mean UFOs," corrected Jason.

"Yeah, same thing! Well it was during the First World War – and you know my experiences there. It was a long, unrelenting, horrific five years and many times I heard accounts of seeing angels."

"Angels?" Jason asked.

"Angels. See, the French, British and Canadian troops all reported incidents where the wounded or dying were aided by the "Comrade in White", "Friend of the Wounded" or "White Helper", Archangel Michael, St George and Archangel Raphael. And of course when you're in a bad state you perhaps begin to imagine things."

"Of course," Jason said.

"In the early years thousands believed that a miracle had happened during the British Expeditionary Force's first desperate clash with the advancing Germans at Mons in Belgium on 23rd August 1914. British forces were fighting a hopeless rearguard action against the Germans with little chance of survival. Outnumbered. Holed up and defeated."

Jason sat forward in his chair with his elbow on his knees, listening intently.

"I heard some say St George and phantom bowmen halted the Kaiser's troops, while others claimed angels had thrown a protective curtain around the British, saving them from disaster. I met this lieutenant, decorated, a very brave and trusted man, Lieutenant Philips he was."

"He described the sighting of the Angel of Mons and reported watching the angel - or rather angels, because there were three of them ranked together - for over 45 minutes. It was around eight o'clock at night. There was a tall central figure flanked closely by two smaller figures on either side."

"Wow!" Jason said mesmerised.

"For himself, and his battalion beside him, it was no mere matter of faith that the angels had protected them: it was a matter of fact. The advancing German forces on the right flank recoiled in disorder. Later Philips told me a German officer verified the story. He reported that he, his men, and their horses were rendered powerless by the force of an apparition."

"I even saw a report in a newspaper that Maud had saved for me. A Brigadier-General Jason Charteris, who in 1925 became a Member of Parliament, wrote to his wife and reported, "...of how the angel of the Lord on the traditional white horse, and clad all in white with flaming sword, faced the advancing Germans at Mons and forbade their further progress..." at least that was what he said."

"Of course some put the story down to propaganda for the reports of the incident coincided with the bad news from the front. With the failure of Haig's forces to break the German army at the first battle of Ypres and the first use of poison gas all adding to the air of gloom and despair, what better way of raising the nation's spirits than a story claiming angels had intervened to save British soldiers from the Hun?"

"Oh I see, perhaps but..." Jason said.

"Whatever the story, true, false or perhaps propaganda, miraculously, the British troops survived and the Angel of Mons had entered the realms of legend. Certainly Lieutenant Philips was unequivocal."

"And you believe it also?" Jason asked.

"Certainly, no doubt about it," then he added, "there are more things in heaven and earth than are dreamt of in your philosophy, Horatio."

"Hamlet!" Jason said recognising the quote.

That evening Jason was left on his own. The aunts had gone to a chapel meeting raising money to repair the organ. The bellows were becoming so noisy that they would often compete and drown out the lustiest of Welsh hymns. Jack had decided to pay Robert a visit. Jason had been invited along, but had preferred to stay at home.

It being Thursday night he turned on the television just before seven and realised that "Top of the Pops" was on. The programme was presented by Jimmy Saville who Jason thought was madder than the moon but harmless for all that. The show was pretty mixed and he realised that he was watching it with fresh eyes and ears.

The show included glam rock stars including Alice Cooper with *'Schools Out'*, Slade and *'Take Me Bak Ome'*, T-Rex with *'Metal Guru'*, David Bowie and *'Starman'* and a guy in a silver suit called Gary Glitter with *'Rock And Roll Parts 1 and 2'* who Jason took an instant dislike to.

He actually remembered seeing Dave Hill, the Slade guitarist, with the weird blond haircut driving a banana-yellow Rolls Royce plated 'YOB 1' in Wolverhampton. Weird!

A couple of pop tracks were played: Michael Jackson's *'Rockin' Robin'* (tweedle ee dee indeed!), and an awful song by Richard Harris' called *'MacArthur Park'* about leaving a cake out in the rain. Jason decided it must have been written as a bet.

They played The Who's *'Join Together'* to a video of Jimmy Saville doing a sponsored cycle ride – perfect music for riding a bike.

A song by a band called Hawkwind called *'Silver Machine'* sounded amazing and the show wrapped up with the debut single *'10538 Overture'* by a band called the Electric Light Orchestra, which Jason thought was a great name for a band.

To his horror Donny Osmond's *'Puppy Love'* was still number one. You can't win them all!

The show played out with an instrumental track called *'Popcorn'* by Hot Butter – which sounded amazing.

Just as the song faded out the front door opened and the aunts arrived back from their meeting.

Maud was fuming about the way the money was to be raised and thought a whist drive was somehow the "devil's own work". Hettie and Emily thought it might be fun and Agnes thought no matter what worked as long as it raised the money. She didn't relish having to get someone to pump the organ with his or her foot if the bellow went.

21. The Show

You Can If You Think You Can
If you think you are beaten, you are
If you think you dare not, you don't
If you want to win but think you can't

It's almost certain you won't
If you think you'll lose, you're lost
For out in the world we find
Success begins with a fellow's will
It's all in the state of the mind

If you think you are outclassed, you are,
You've got to think high to rise,
You've got to be sure of yourself before
You can ever win a prize.

Life's battles don't always go
To the stronger or faster man.
But sooner or later the man who wins,
Is the man who thinks he can.

C. W. Longenecker

 ith time marching on the end of Jason's holiday at Ty Angylion was fast coming to a close and Jack had been discussing with Jason how it could be ended with style. "With a bang! So to speak," Jack said.

One afternoon while Robert was sharing his experiences in Germany with Jason and Jack, the subject of Jason's return home was raised.

"Well we must do something?" Robert said.

"Agreed but what?" Jack said.

"What about a show?" Jason said.

"A show?" Robert asked, "What sort of show?"

"I think I know where he's coming from on this one!" Jack said.

And as a chorus the three cried "Shakespeare!"

They agreed that they would put together perhaps an hour of readings and speeches. Speeches that were well known and if they didn't know the speeches by heart they could just read them out.

They began to brainstorm what should be included.

"Hamlet – To be!" Jack said.

"All the world's a stage!" Robert said.

"Blow Winds – from Lear!" Jason said.

"Is there something we could do together?" Robert asked.

"Oh, yes!" Jack said smiling, "We could do the Three Witches from Macbeth!"

"Great idea," Robert said.

After half an hour they had put together a programme of extracts. At first it would have been two hours long, but Jack and Robert, who knew many of the speeches, cut this down to a more manageable 60 minutes.

As they only had two copies of the Complete Works of Shakespeare Richard popped home for his copy and within an hour rehearsals had begun.

As each speech was read by one of them, the others would suggest different approaches and inflection – directing the actor – such that the impact would be greater.

By half past five the first read-through had been completed in just over an hour.

"Perfect time," Jack said, "it may be a tad longer but about the right length."

"Could I do a programme?" Jason said.

"Oh yes, capital idea," Robert said, "if you do it on a sheet of paper both sides folded in half like a book I'll get it photocopied"

"But what shall we call it?" Jack said.

"What about 'Shakespeare's Greatest Hits'," Jason suggested. Jack and Robert burst out laughing. "Not good?" Jason said thinking he'd made a faux pas. "No, very good in fact," Robert said. "Shakespeare's Greatest Hits sounds very upbeat."

So it was that over the following days the content and programme were refined and a date of the final Saturday of Jason's stay was agreed for the performance to take place.

With this decision made Jason could now complete the draft of the paper programme. On the front page he had drawn a cartoon of Shakespeare wearing cool sunglasses. He added the show's title underneath. The names of the actors were placed on the following page in alphabetical order – Jack Hughes, Jason Hughes and Robert Hawthorne. On the third page the list of speeches was split by an interval, "So we can have a drink of water," Jack said.

After taking advice from Robert and Jack about what to put on the back page Jason added some silly credits like 'Cakes by Maud', 'Tea by Hettie', 'Toilet Rolls by Andrex' and he also added a dedication – 'With Love to Clarrie'.

The following day the draft was approved and Robert took it away to print enough copies.

"Ten should be enough," Robert said. "Ten?" Jason asked, "There's only four aunts."

"Oh yes, but we've invited a couple of friends to enjoy the evening," Jack said.

"Don't worry Jason, you know them – Reverend Pastor Bryn Evans, the people next door – it will be fine!" Robert said.

Jason shrugged, they were right. It would be fine but he resolved that he must be word perfect in the short speeches he had learned. Especially Hamlet's 'To be...' speech – Jack's so called "biggy" and there were a couple of others which he wanted to shine at but time was short.

Saturday night came around very quickly and soon he was helping to move the furniture such that the lounge was laid out to seat about ten.

The double doors of the dining room were swung backwards to create the arch of the stage.

Agnes hung it with two old velvet curtains, which could be pulled back at the start and end of the speeches.

At seven o'clock the guests began to arrive and took their seats. The Reverend and his wife, the next-door neighbours, the Griffiths and all the aunts.

At seven-thirty Agnes switched off the lights and the curtain was pulled back to reveal Jack who began with the opening Chorus speech from Henry V – "O for a muse of fire".

This warmed the audience up and then a series of short pieces from the histories were performed.

Robert did a couple of speeches from Richard III including "Now is the winter":

Now is the winter of our discontent
Made glorious summer by this sun of York;
And all the clouds that lour'd upon our house
In the deep bosom of the ocean buried.
Now are our brows bound with victorious wreaths;
Our bruised arms hung up for monuments;
Our stern alarums changed to merry meetings,
Our dreadful marches to delightful measures.
Grim-visaged war hath smooth'd his wrinkled front;
And now, instead of mounting barded steeds
To fright the souls of fearful adversaries,
He capers nimbly in a lady's chamber
To the lascivious pleasing of a lute.

Robert smiled his most evil and mischievous of grins:

But I, that am not shaped for sportive tricks,
Nor made to court an amorous looking-glass;
I, that am rudely stamp'd, and want love's majesty
To strut before a wanton ambling nymph;
I, that am curtail'd of this fair proportion,
Cheated of feature by dissembling nature,
Deformed, unfinish'd, sent before my time
Into this breathing world, scarce half made up,
And that so lamely and unfashionable

126

> *That dogs bark at me as I halt by them;*
> *Why, I, in this weak piping time of peace,*
> *Have no delight to pass away the time,*
> *Unless to spy my shadow in the sun*
> *And descant on mine own deformity:*
> *And therefore, since I cannot prove a lover,*
> *To entertain these fair well-spoken days,*
> *I am determined to prove a villain*

and "A horse, a horse";

> *...I have set my life upon a cast,*
> *And I will stand the hazard of the die:*
> *I think there be six Richmond's in the field;*
> *Five have I slain to-day instead of him.*
> *A horse! a horse! my kingdom for a horse!*

Jason then did the Richmond speech from the same play, which completes the cycle:

> *All this divided York and Lancaster,*
> *Divided in their dire division,*
> *O, now, let Richmond and Elizabeth,*
> *The true succeeders of each royal house,*
> *By God's fair ordinance conjoin together!*

Jack read the speech by Mortimer from Henry VI Part 1, which explained the Plantagenet family tree:

> *Henry the Fourth, grandfather to this king,*
> *Deposed his nephew Richard, Edward's son,*
> *The first begotten and the lawful heir,*
> *Of Edward king, the third of that descent:*
> *During whose reign the Percies of the north,*
> *Finding his usurpation most unjust,*
> *Endeavor'd my advancement to the throne:*
> *The reason moved these warlike lords to this*
> *Was, for that - young King Richard thus removed,*
> *Leaving no heir begotten of his body -*
> *I was the next by birth and parentage;*

For by my mother I derived am

Then Jack and Jason did a piece from Henry IV with young Hal and Falstaff:

PRINCE HENRY
Didst thou never see Titan kiss a dish of butter?
pitiful-hearted Titan, that melted at the sweet tale
of the sun's! if thou didst, then behold that compound.

FALSTAFF
You rogue, here's lime in this sack too: there is
nothing but roguery to be found in villainous man:
yet a coward is worse than a cup of sack with lime
in it. A villainous coward! Go thy ways, old Jack;
die when thou wilt, if manhood, good manhood, be
not forgot upon the face of the earth, then am I a
shotten herring. There live not three good men
unhanged in England; and one of them is fat and
grows old: God help the while! a bad world, I say.
I would I were a weaver; I could sing psalms or any
thing. A plague of all cowards, I say still.

PRINCE HENRY
How now, wool-sack! what mutter you?

FALSTAFF
A king's son! If I do not beat thee out of thy
kingdom with a dagger of lath, and drive all thy
subjects afore thee like a flock of wild-geese,
I'll never wear hair on my face more. You Prince of Wales!

PRINCE HENRY
Why, you whoreson round man, what's the matter?

This caused much laughter from the audience and they wrapped up the section with Jason reading the St Crispin's day speech from Henry V.

This day is called the feast of Crispian:

128

He that outlives this day, and comes safe home,
Will stand a tip-toe when the day is named,
And rouse him at the name of Crispian.
He that shall live this day, and see old age,
Will yearly on the vigil feast his neighbours,
And say 'To-morrow is Saint Crispian:'
Then will he strip his sleeve and show his scars.
And say 'These wounds I had on Crispin's day.'
Old men forget: yet all shall be forgot,
But he'll remember with advantages
What feats he did that day: then shall our names.
Familiar in his mouth as household words
Harry the king, Bedford and Exeter,
Warwick and Talbot, Salisbury and Gloucester,
Be in their Flowing cups freshly remember'd.
This story shall the good man teach his son;
And Crispin Crispian shall ne'er go by,
From this day to the ending of the world,
But we in it shall be remember'd;
We few, we happy few, we band of brothers;
For he to-day that sheds his blood with me
Shall be my brother; be he ne'er so vile,
This day shall gentle his condition:
And gentlemen in England now a-bed
Shall think themselves accursed they were not here,
And hold their manhood's cheap whiles any speaks
That fought with us upon Saint Crispin's day.

There was great applause and they returned to finish the first half
with Robert reading 'All the world's a stage' from 'As You Like it':

All the world's a stage,
And all the men and women merely players;
They have their exits and their entrances,
And one man in his time plays many parts,
His acts being seven ages. At first, the infant,
Mewling and puking in the nurse's arms.
Then the whining schoolboy, with his satchel

And shining morning face, creeping like snail
Unwillingly to school. And then the lover,
Sighing like furnace, with a woeful ballad
Made to his mistress' eyebrow. Then a soldier,
Full of strange oaths and bearded like the pard,
Jealous in honor, sudden and quick in quarrel,
Seeking the bubble reputation
Even in the cannon's mouth. And then the justice,
In fair round belly with good capon lined,
With eyes severe and beard of formal cut,
Full of wise saws and modern instances;
And so he plays his part. The sixth age shifts
Into the lean and slippered pantaloon,
With spectacles on nose and pouch on side;
His youthful hose, well saved, a world too wide
For his shrunk shank, and his big manly voice,
Turning again towards childish treble, pipes
And whistles in his sound. Last scene of all,
That ends this strange eventful history,
Is second childishness and mere oblivion,
Sans teeth, sans eyes, sans taste, sans everything.

There was poignancy in the speech and the audience fell silent for a few seconds as they reflected on the words.

Jack then performed "If music be the food of love" from "Twelfth Night":

If music be the food of love, play on;
Give me excess of it, that, surfeiting,
The appetite may sicken, and so die.
That strain again;--it had a dying fall;
O, it came o'er my ear like the sweet south,
That breathes upon a bank of violets,
Stealing and giving odour.

Jason closed the first half reading Sonnet 116:

Let me not to the marriage of true minds
Admit impediments. Love is not love
Which alters when it alteration finds,

130

> *Or bends with the remover to remove:*
> *O no! it is an ever-fixed mark*
> *That looks on tempests and is never shaken;*
> *It is the star to every wandering bark,*
> *Whose worth's unknown, although his height be taken.*
> *Love's not Time's fool, though rosy lips and cheeks*
> *Within his bending sickle's compass come:*
> *Love alters not with his brief hours and weeks,*
> *But bears it out even to the edge of doom.*
> *If this be error and upon me proved,*
> *I never writ, nor no man ever loved.*

Again there was much applause followed by an extended interval where Robert, Jack and Jason joined the audience for nibbles, cheese and pineapple, crisps, peanuts and wine.

"Wine?" the Reverend asked Maud, somewhat surprised and teasing her.

"I don't believe its written anywhere as being a sin?" she replied, "In fact Jesus drank it on a number of occasions."

Bryn-Evans smiled, "Indeed he did!"

"A fine performance young man," Mr Griffiths told Jason, "you have a talent."

"Thank you," Jason said humbly and Robert interjected, "A very strong talent which both Jack and I hope he will cultivate."

Then after almost half an hour Jack clapped his hands twice to gain attention. "Ladies and gentlemen. If music be the food of love, we must play on!"

The lights were turned off again and the curtains pulled back. The second half was to be tragedies and Jason, Robert and Jack lit their faces with three torches making themselves look very evil as they read the witches' speech from Macbeth – 'when will we three meet again.'

This was followed by Jack's 'Blow Winds' speech from Lear with Jason chipping in the lines for the Fool. Then Robert performed the Mark Anthony speech from Julius Caesar 'I come to bury Caesar not to praise him':

> *I come to bury Caesar, not to praise him.*
> *The evil that men do lives after them;*
> *the good is oft interred with their bones.*

Then Jack gave a big build-up for Jason, rather more like a showman than a Shakespearean actor.

"Ladeees and Gentlemen!" he said like a circus master, "And now, without aid of safety net or harness of any kind…" and he paused for dramatic effect, "…our very own… Hamlet."

The same torches were used to illuminate Jason's face from the side as he performed the 'To be or not to be' speech.

At the end of the speech there was a moment of reflective thought and then the audience clapped loudly. Jason bowed and the show continued to its close.

Robert gave them the closing speech from Romeo and Juliet:

> *For never was a story of more woe*
> *Than this of Juliet and her Romeo.*

Jack the closing lines from Hamlet:

> *Let four captains*
> *Bear Hamlet, like a soldier, to the stage;*
> *For he was likely, had he been put on,*
> *To have proved most royally: and, for his passage,*
> *The soldiers' music and the rites of war*
> *Speak loudly for him.*
> *Take up the bodies: such a sight as this*
> *Becomes the field, but here shows much amiss.*
> *Go, bid the soldiers shoot.*

Jason finished with Puck's final lines from Midsummer's Night Dream:

> *If we shadows have offended,*
> *Think but this, and all is mended,*
> *That you have but slumber'd here*
> *While these visions did appear.*
> *And this weak and idle theme,*
> *No more yielding but a dream,*
> *Gentles, do not reprehend:*
> *if you pardon, we will mend:*
> *And, as I am an honest Puck,*
> *If we have unearned luck*
> *Now to 'scape the serpent's tongue,*
> *We will make amends ere long;*
> *Else the Puck a liar call;*
> *So, good night unto you all.*
> *Give me your hands, if we be friends,*
> *And Robin shall restore amends.*

In response to Puck's request the audience clapped again and stood shouting "Bravo, Bravo!" loudly as Jason, Robert and Jack bowed smiling like Cheshire Cats.

It was in this moment of acceptance, feeling the warmth of enjoyment from the audience that Jason realised that this was what he enjoyed; that perhaps he might be born for acting; a career that six weeks previously he would have never considered.

The curtains were pulled back and the lights went on and there were many handshakes and "Well dones".

Then Jack spoke, "Ladies and gentlemen I hope you have enjoyed this one-off performance of 'Shakespeare's Greatest Hits'. I believe tonight you have seen the debut of a new star," and he put a hand on Jason's shoulder, "Robert and I are convinced he will go far and perhaps one day we will see him at the National or the Royal Shakespeare." This was followed by claps of agreement and exclamations of "Bravo!".

"Tonight you saw him begin to apprentice his craft to an audience. Along the way he will gather more tools for his trade. There is one which I would like to present." And Agnes handed Jack a parcel wrapped in golden wrapping paper.

"For you Jason," Jack said handing it to him. It looked like a birthday present and the label on it said "To Jason from his fans".

Jason sat down and opened it, tearing off a corner. Inside was a brand new leather-bound copy of "The Complete Works of Shakespeare". He opened the front cover and saw it was signed by each of the aunts, Jack, and Robert.

Jason was speechless and struggling for words, choking with emotion all he could blurt out was, "Thank you. You're very kind." And again he was drowned in hugs and handshakes.

As the Griffiths and Bryn-Evans' went home Jason stayed behind on the sofa flicking the thin pages of the volume. It was a beautiful book, quite heavy and contained paintings of various Pre-Raphaelite paintings including Two Gentlemen of Verona and Ophelia.

Then he was re-joined by Robert, Jack and the aunts.

"Well young man, off to bed with you I think. A big day tomorrow," Maud said.

"Yes, you're right I have quite a collection to take home," Jason replied.

"Your mum said that they would be here for lunch and then leave soon after. They'll just do a day trip," Agnes said.

Jason smiled then said, "I must be honest. When I was told I was coming here I dreaded it. I felt I was being passed on like a parcel. But you have shown such kindness, such generosity, such love that I will be very, very sad to go."

And in turn he kissed each one of the aunts and then shook Robert's and Jack's hand.

"Have a good sleep lad," Jack said, "see you in the morning"

"Yes, good night all, and thanks again," he said and then carrying his book under his arm he climbed the long flight of stairs to his bedroom once more and perhaps for a final time, at least during this stay.

In his room he had already begun to gather the many things he had been given and Maud had left his case next to his record player, which was already packed up.

He walked to the window to close the curtains and gazed over the wonderful view, which doubtless he would miss.

As he did so he looked out over the estuary and over towards the twinkling lights of Borth in the distance. The sight of glimmering white and orange through the night haze matched that of the evening.

Absolutely magical.

22. Going Home

"Treat the earth well:
it was not given to you by your parents,
it was loaned to you by your children.
We do not inherit the Earth from our Ancestors,
we borrow it from our Children".

The next morning at eight o'clock before breakfast, as was tradition, the aunts, Jack and Jason walked from Ty Angylion through the town to the chapel and were greeted by Reverend Bryn-Evans, whose smile lit up the coldest Sunday morning and who even though he had seen them the previous evening greeted them as if it had been years.

"Perhaps your last time for a little while?" Bryn-Evans asked Jason.

"Yes, I'm afraid so," Jason said in agreement.

"I think we have something special this morning," Bryn-Evans said and the congregation began filling the hall as the golden sunshine beamed through the chapel windows.

The opening hymn was 'All Things Bright and Beautiful' – Clarrie's favourite and the aunts smiled as Agnes played the opening bars of the song. Then Bryn-Evans gave the sermon; his theme was children and love and his text was again from Corinthians.

1 Corinthians 13:4-8
4 Love is patient, love is kind.
It does not envy, it does not boast, it is not proud.
5 It does not dishonour others, it is not self-seeking, it is not easily
angered, it keeps no record of wrongs.
6 Love does not delight in evil but rejoices with the truth.
7 It always protects, always trusts, always hopes, always perseveres.
8. Love never fails.

Then he spoke the final verse with emphasis: "But always remember throughout your lives Verse 8: Love never fails," he said smiling and in that moment Jason thought it was a message for him.

The service ended and the church emptied out into the warming morning air.

Bryn-Evans shook hands with Jason, "I don't know why Jason," he said, "but I feel that Verse 8 – love never fails – should be your creed. As well as many others of course. Remember it as you grow into a young man." He smiled and shook Jason's hand warmly.

The aunts walked slowly back to the house, with Jack and Jason walking behind with Robert.

"So have you enjoyed your summer in Aberdovey?" Robert said.

"Immensely," Jason said, "I can't believe what I've seen, what I've learned. The kindness."

"Will you remember it?" Robert asked.

"Of course. As long as I live. How could I not?" Jason replied.

"It been…," and Jack searched for a word, "…fun!" "It's been great fun," he said unequivocally.

"It has Uncle Jack," Jason agreed. "We lost one along the way of course."

"Oh, I'm sure she's been watching and smiling with us these last few weeks," Jack replied, referring to Clarrie.

They arrived at the house and Maud and Hettie set about cooking a special breakfast. This morning they were treating everyone to pork chops, eggs and gravy.

"Father's favourite Sunday breakfast!" Hettie said.

"Besides, you'll need something for the journey," Maud added.

Within half an hour, the table was laid and with Robert joining them the big breakfast was served.

"This will certainly set us up for the day!" Jack said.

"For the week!" Jason said, patting his belly.

After breakfast Jason was given furlough together with Jack and Robert to bring his things down from the bedroom.

There were his case, books including the Complete Works, magazines, the photo album, record player, a few records plus a few classical records Agnes had given him. A large pile accumulated by the front door ready to be packed in the car when his parents arrived.

"Got a car load there," Robert said, "you got everything?"

"I'd better go and check," Jason replied, and he shot back up the stairs.

He got to the bedroom and found Agnes sitting on the bed. She turned and smiled as he walked through the door.

"It's going to quiet without you," she said, her eyes filling with tears.

Jason hugged her, "Don't be sad. I'll write and I'm sure we'll see each other at Christmas won't we?"

"Yes. I know, I've just enjoyed showing you the things I would have shown my children if I could have had them," she said, a hint of sadness in her voice.

"I've enjoyed it too," Jason said, "and we can write can't we?"

"Good idea," she said standing up, "you can tell me how things are going at school. Are you looking forward to the new school year?"

Jason smiled, "Yes, for the first time in my life I think I know what I want to do. I've got lots of ideas. I think it's going to be a special year."

"I'm sure it will." She kissed his head, "Now you have a quick check in case you've forgotten anything," and with that she went down the stairs.

Jason was left in the now silent room with a cool breeze off the bay blowing the curtains. He looked around for a final time. He'd already checked the drawers and wardrobe, and then he looked out the window one last time. He was going to miss the view, that was for sure. He sighed, and then followed his aunt down the stairs.

The rest of the morning was spent over in the park reading the Sunday papers and enjoying the conversations and banter of his aunts and their plans.

As he watched them talk it struck him that none of them were getting any younger. He looked at Agnes who was laughing and joking with Robert. Perhaps theirs was a relationship which would grow and blossom again with time. They did seem very close and good together.

Maud and Hettie were as intense as ever; discussing the Sunday service, the quality of the meat at the supermarket, the state of the town at the end of the summer when the tourists had all gone. It was as if they gained energy from each other's annoyances.

Emily sat as usual knitting quietly without fuss and bother, just listening to the noise, chat and bustle around her. Her sight was getting much worse but her knitting she could do in her sleep.

Jack smoked his pipe and watched the boats in the estuary, reflecting on the moments in his life that ebb and flow like the tide in the bay.

Jason would remember and miss them all, as well as these moments of closeness and belonging.

At around one o'clock his parents arrived and parked their car just under the Penhelig railway bridge.

His mother greeted him with a hug and the usual question as to whether he had been behaving. His father acknowledged him but there was no real affection – it was his wife's responsibility to show love.

"I hope Jason has not been too much trouble?" he asked Maud.

"Jason has been no trouble at all," Maud said, "we're going to be very sad to see him go."

"That's a surprise," he said, a hint of sarcasm in his voice, "he's usually up to something or another."

"We didn't find that at all. Very polite and quite a character," Hettie said.

His father realised he was fighting a losing battle. "Well we can't stay long – we have a four-hour drive back," he said.

"Well, we've prepared some tea and sandwiches," Hettie said, "we'll bring them over to the park. We have blankets and some deckchairs laid out already."

Over tea and sandwiches Jason told his Mum about his time in Aberdovey. About his record player, his records, his walks, his time with Uncle Jack, the show, and the words gushed from him like a fountain.

"You sound like you've lived the life of Riley," his Mum said, "Are you sure you want to come home?"

Jason knew it was a loaded question but he replied diplomatically, "Of course I do – I've missed you and I'm really looking forward to school."

He father heard this and interjected. "I should hope so. I want to see some hard work out of you next year."

Jack darted at look at Jason's father. "You know, with a little less criticism and more positive encouragement Jason could do very well. I hope you remember this in the coming years. "

His father was a little taken aback by Jack's comment, "Of course, he's a bright lad but needs to put in the effort."

"There's more to growing up than money and work you know," Jack said.

His father didn't reply, there was nothing to say.

With his family duties fulfilled he turned to Jason. "Come on young man, we should be getting on our way." And handing him the car keys he indicated that Jason should put his things in the boot.

Jason, Robert and Jack crossed the road and loaded the car. Jason's things fitted easily in the boot. Just as it was about to close Jason picked up the Complete Works from the box he'd been given and put it on the back seat to read on the way home.

Jason handed back the car keys and his father put them in his pocket, "Done?" his father asked. Jason nodded.

"Come on Irene," he called to his wife, "we're ready."

Jason's Mum broke off her conversation and the round of farewells began.

Eventually Jason's father had started the car and turned it around so it was parked over the entrance to the jetty out of the traffic.

"Come on Jason, get a move on," his father said, "say your goodbyes – we've got a long drive ahead of us."

And so Jason hugged and kissed each one of his aunts and he could see each of them becoming gradually more emotional.

Robert shook his hand warmly. "Now you be sure to cultivate and grow that talent of yours."

Then Jack took the same hand. "In the words of the bard – parting is such sweet sorrow!"

Jason smiled broadly and said, "Thank you Uncle Jack. It's been…, well…, great!"

Then getting into the car he said, "I hope I can come again next year?" and as the car pulled away there were shouts of "Of course" and "Goodbye".

Jason looked out of the car window and saw them all gathered on the pavement waving as the car turned the corner up the coast road.

No sooner had they set off or his father and mother began to argue about this and that; about the best route home, if they should stop for tea, what had everyone said about Jason's behaviour; normally Jason would have listened intently, occasionally cringing or expecting a tell-off for some indiscretion or misbehaviour; on this occasion he tuned it all out as if listening to a radio and realised it had become mere sounds and murmurs.

Jason sighed and turned to his left where his copy of "The Complete Works of Shakespeare" lay on the next seat.

He placed a hand on it and felt the gold engraving on the cover, his fingers tracing the words in the title. It was as if to do so would conjure up the book's magical, potent and special energy.

He smiled and was comforted by it; it was one thing that they could never take away from him, or sully or destroy.

The car approached a long curving bend, turned the corner and Jason felt he had just done the same.

23. Ready for School

The Secret Garden

*In each century since the beginning of the world
wonderful things have been discovered.
In the last century more amazing things were found out
than in any century before.*

Frances Hodgson Burnett

*T*he days after Jason returned home were filled with preparing for his new school term. Shoes had to be polished, clothes to be checked and if necessary repaired, and finally new clothes had to be bought. This, however, was a rarity and the only allowance this year was a new tie as Jason had spilt ink on his old one.

By Friday everything was ready and Jason found time to write a letter thanking the aunts and Jack for having taken good care of him.

He was looking forward to the new school year and felt that he should widen his interests outside schoolwork. His parents would be concerned by this of course; his mother in case it distracted him from his school work and his father in case it cost him more money.

One decision he had made was that he wanted to have a weekend job, perhaps on a Saturday, to earn a little money. Since his parents didn't give him any pocket money he'd need some financial support from somewhere else if he wanted to be able to pursue other interests.

Luckily his friend helped on a farm, which was only a short walk away from where Jason lived and they were always looking for help on a Saturday morning.

After a short and cursory interview he agreed with the farmer to work for £1.90 per hour for four hours every Saturday morning, "cash in hand".

For Jason this was a small fortune and for the first time in his life he felt financially independent. He told his parents about his new job, but they weren't really bothered; his father brought up the subject of housekeeping and perhaps Jason contributing if he was earning, but for once his Mum stepped in and told his father not to be ridiculous.

Jason had worked out that within a couple of weeks he would be able to buy a second-hand bike such that he could cycle to his job and visit friends, then perhaps he could save and even buy the occasional LP and who knows, maybe even go to his first rock concert if he could ever afford it.

Since his time in Aberdovey Jason's first thought was to join an amateur dramatic society and get involved with drama and acting at school. Most of the school performances were usually musicals such as 'West Side Story', 'Oliver', 'Oklahoma', 'My Fair Lady' – that sort of thing, but he would like to experience acting in front of a real audience. One of his options to expand his knowledge of classic works was to take English Literature rather than Biology and he decided that it would be a great idea.

He also thought he should do more sport – at the end of the previous term he had tried hockey and really enjoyed it. He'd also like to try badminton and tennis. His school was lucky enough and big enough to have good sports facilities so he knew he would have the opportunity.

All in all he was getting very excited about the new school year and for the first time he had a feeling in his stomach that something great was about to happen, a new opportunity or a new door opening.

His own parents' situation had gone to the back of his mind and he had not really dwelt on it nor had his parents raised it since he had returned.

He realized also he would probably have the distraction of girls – both of his friends now had girlfriends and though he didn't think too much about it he knew that perhaps he would probably end up with a girlfriend in the new school year.

It seemed to him inevitable but he was quite ambivalent to the possibility. If it happened, and he believed it would, it happened.

He also decided to change his bedroom around. He wanted to create more space and also have room for a desk and chair to work from. In the past he had worked at the kitchen or dining room table, which was not very productive and always led to interruptions. He pushed the bed to the wall, instantly creating more floor space.

In the garage he found a lone and battered kitchen table, which he rescued. He reinforced its broken leg with a splint of wood screwed over the break. This was a little rough but a perfect size for a desk. He then borrowed a dining chair to sit upon. He put the record player on the desk and realised he would be able to play music while he worked.

He also put up the posters he'd had on his wall at Ty Angylion and then created a library on the fireplace with his books and since the fireplace was never used he stacked his albums on its floor.

At the end of the day he stood back and admired his work. He nodded, pleased with the transformation; definitely an improvement and now more like a student's study than a child's play room.

He also tidied his wardrobes and cleared out some of the clothes that he never wore or that were too small and put them in a bin bag. He placed the bag in the hall and just said, "Charity!" to his Mum and went back to his room.

By the Saturday evening he was ready for the following week and he felt something churning like butterflies in his stomach.

There was something that he couldn't put his finger on but it felt like an excitement, a tingling of anticipation, which he'd only known once before on the night when Jack, Robert and he had performed "Shakespeare's Greatest Hits" – it was the feeling that you got just before you were to go on stage.

Jason absolutely relished it.

24. Fresh Fields

I don't believe in destiny
Or the guiding hand of fate
I don't believe in forever
Or love as a mystical state
I don't believe in the stars or the planets
Or angels watching from above
But I believe there's a ghost of a chance we can find someone to love
And make it last...

T he following week Jason started back at school and the first few days were spent in induction; the school had been radically reorganised and re-streamed and two other, smaller schools had been integrated into his such that now in his third year his class and year were slightly different.

As a result he had fifteen new classmates, girls and boys from other schools now within his class. His form and subject teachers were introduced and he made a number of subject choices – Maths and English and Physical Ed' were mandatory but as he hoped he could do Music and Drama as one option and English Literature as another.

His parents had wanted him to do pure sciences but given his previous years he neither had the aptitude nor the interest in Chemistry, Physics or Biology. He also joined a number of clubs and societies within the school including of course Drama, Hockey and Tennis, which, given the size of the school, were never oversubscribed.

The year seemed to have a different flavour; more focussed and academic than the previous years. There was the definite feeling of endeavour and hard work for the coming year.

During his second week Jason attended the first meeting of the Drama Group, which was held after school. This first meeting was a brainstorm of ideas as to which performances they would give during the coming year. The drama head was insistent that a show be performed and "Oliver" had already been earmarked. The music teacher wanted to do a "Songs from the Shows" evening but initial ideas for pure drama were lacking.

Jason suggested something by Shakespeare, which was initially groaned at, but he replayed the "Greatest Hits" idea from his time at Ty Angylion and this was pencilled in with some changes.

A couple of murder mysteries were suggested, which everyone agreed could be dire, but finally everyone settled on to J.B. Priestley's 'An Inspector Calls'. "A small cast, very little scenery and with a moral message" one of the group said.

Then the drama teacher said, "I'd like to do a warm-up evening of poetry readings. We each take a copy of the 'Quiller Couch Oxford Book of Poetry' and choose three short poems to do." Then she paired the girls off with the boys to choose their selection. "Twenty minutes," she said and they got started.

Jason turned to the girl next to him; she was as tall as he was, and quite slim with blond hair and wearing John Lennon glasses. She was sucking a fruit lolly.

"Hi, I'm Jason," he said.

"Francis," she said rolling the lolly in her mouth and then shaking his hand then said, "So what do you think? Any ideas?"

She had an air of rebellion about her; her uniform was worn loosely - thrown on rather than put on - as if she didn't really feel the necessity to show any pretensions. Most of the girls wore their skirts short, hers was long - maxi; most of the girls wore their blouses buttoned at the cuff; her sleeves were rolled up. Her tie was worn like a bootlace tied in a reef knot. She wanted to make a statement.

"I don't know," Jason said, "I don't know the book at all; shall we just scan through?"

And sharing a single copy of the book they skipped through the list of poems at the front, occasionally spotting a poet they knew.

"No Shakespeare!" Francis said firmly. "Ok. No Shakespeare!" Jason agreed, "Just this once."

Francis smiled, "You some kind of swot wanting to do Bill Shakes? Very courageous I thought suggesting it," she said teasing him.

"No. It's just someone taught me how to read his works. How to bring them to life," he replied.

"Nah! You'd need 4000 volts to bring some of them to life," she replied and they both laughed. "I know; let's go through the index kind of at random; any poets I recognise I shout them out and if you know them as well we'll choose."

"OK," Francis said taking out a notepad and biro, "sounds like a plan." And she pushed her glasses up her nose. Jason watched her as she did this and noticed her eyes were greyish-green.

"OK, here goes," Jason said and began to read from the index. "Walt Whitman, Shelley, Christina Rossetti, Tennyson, Browning, Wordsworth, Bryon, Coleridge, Yeats…" and he paused, "how are we doing?"

"Good, agree with most of those. Defo' for Walt Whitman. Except for Christina Rossetti. Who's she?" Francis asked.

"A romantic poet I think – Pre-Raphaelite from the late 19th century – I remember my aunt reading a couple of her poems," Jason replied.

"Ok, lover boy eh?" and with a smirk she winked at him. "Sounds ok. We'll put her on the list," she said.

"Er… Did you just wink at me?" Jason asked.

"No. No. Definitely not," Francis replied lying very badly and attempting to back pedal.

"Okay, I'll take your word for it," Jason said smiling.

That evening Jason walked Francis home, a little out of his way but he thought it was worth it.

"Thanks for the help with the poems," Francis said, "it was good fun."

"Yeah, I enjoyed it too," Jason replied then he thought for a moment.

"Look I heard the drama teacher say that she was thinking of organising a trip over to Stratford-upon-Avon to see a play during the next few weeks. Would you fancy going together?" he asked and then couldn't think of where the last sentence had originated.

Francis smiled widely, "Jason? Are you asking me on a date?"

"Well, I... no, but, yes but..." Then taking a breath he said, "Ok. Yes I am."

"Then I accept," Francis said and smiling she turned around, and with a skip in her step went into her house. She waved as she closed the door.

Jason stood for a moment and it occurred to him that something had definitely happened and then he realised that he probably now had a girlfriend.

"Cool!" he said smiling and nodding to himself. "Cool..." and walked back up the street to go home. As he did for no reason a thought entered his head, a memory of the sermon Reverend Bryn Evans had given on Jason's last Sunday in Aberdovey. "First Book of Corinthians. Chapter 13. Verse 8. What was it? Love never fails," he remembered and then said it out loud and hitching his bag over his shoulder continued his journey home.

So it was that the summer of 1972 was the start of many things for Jason. His first love, his first job, his first acting performance, indeed a host of new experiences that engulfed him during the following year and on into his teenage years which would have a profound effect on his journey into adulthood.

25. A New Quest

The golden moments in the stream of life rush past us
and we see nothing but sand;
the angels come to visit us,
and we only know them when they're gone.

George Eliot

O ver the next few years the aunts and Jack wrote to Jason regularly and indeed he would visit and stay every year, usually for two weeks in the summer and a week at Easter.

Every few weeks the aunts would send him a pack of letters, organized by Agnes and written by some or all of the aunts and Jack depending on how busy they were.

Jason would reply as and when he could with an open letter addressed to all. He would tell of his new experiences, his work, his acting and drama, how he was progressing in school and outside of it.

Francis and he became very close and the following summer they decided to cycle some 140 miles across Wales, with two stops from Wolverhampton to Ludlow then from Ludlow to Rhayader, then onto Aberdovey staying in youth hostels. The trip was a memorable one, not least for the rain on one day when rather than getting drenched they threw both bikes on the Devil's Bridge railway to save the uphill ride and keep dry. The cost of two singles with bikes was well worth it. It was the first of many holidays together.

Then Emily, who was now 84 and very frail, passed late in January of 1975. It was said just of old age.

Agnes and Robert, both in their late 70s, had also become an item and married in the summer of 1976. Jason and Francis attended both the service in the chapel and the reception that followed, both small affairs, and Jason was asked to read Sonnet 123.

Jason was gratified to witness that love and companionship could be found at any age.

Not long after Agnes and Robert were married Hettie grew very ill with angina. Her illness was short and in the October of 1976 she succumbed and passed away, aged 75.

Agnes and Robert both lived for another seven years with Robert passing first and Agnes a few months later. It was as if on his death Agnes just gave up to join him.

Maud lived to the ripe old age of 90. In her last few years she lived in a residential home just outside Aberdovey and when she died all those who lived there missed her. To pay for her care 'Ty Angylion' was sold and passed outside the family.

Jack's energy remained boundless and he occasionally rang Jason when the mood took him to talk of this and that, mainly Shakespeare of course, and acting and drama. Jason realized that Jack's dream of being an actor lived on in him and for that he had no problem carrying that particular torch.

In 1977, aged 18, Jason left school with three A Levels in English, English Literature and History and went to Warwick University where he studied English and gained a Bachelor of Arts.

From 1973 through his university years he was active in drama and acting and appeared in many productions, in fact, as many as he could manage. At one time he had four production rehearsals going on and found the challenge of juggling learning lines and characterization exhilarating.

The month before he graduated he had applied for entry into a number of drama schools including the Guildhall, RADA and the London School and was interviewed by each.

In the May of 1980 he received two letters, one from his Uncle Jack and the other from Guildhall. He had already received rejections from RADA and London so he had low expectations.

Jason elected to open the letter from Jack first – he was never disappointed by the content of a letter from Jack.

Jack, who was now well into his 83rd year, wrote:

"To think that when you're gone there is more than oblivion is somehow comforting, that while your spirit might be gone there is something of you left on this earth. Perhaps only in thoughts and ideas, or words on a page or something more tangible in wood, stone or steel. In whatever way they are your offspring and outlive you.

I read something by Richard David Bach the other day about one's mission on earth. It said, "Here is a test to find whether your mission on earth is finished: If you're alive, it isn't." I feel my mission is accomplished and coming to a close.

That you have achieved what you have makes me very proud not only as your Great Uncle but as a friend. I therefore offer this small gift to help you through whichever drama school you choose."

To Jason's astonishment a cheque for £5,000 was attached to the letter, made payable to him, enough to pay his enrolment fees and accommodation for the first year. Jason slumped speechless on the bed in his student digs, holding the cheque between his hands. He felt emotion swelling within him and put the letter aside and opened the second. The Guildhall stamp was clear on the seal and he felt his heart race as he gently tore the envelope open.

Dear Mr Hughes,

We have great pleasure in accepting you as a student at the Guildhall School for Dramatic Art for the 1980/81 intake.

Term begins on September 15th and we look forward to seeing you then. Please ensure fees....

Yours etc etc..

Jason held up both letters and held them to his chest and thought his heart was going to burst with joy.

"Thank you," he said to no one in particular, "thank you."

A few days after Jason received the letter, Jack died. It was as if he had known that he had little time, and gifting the money was an act of someone desperate to leave a legacy. Jason becoming an actor fulfilled Jack's own ambitions as well as Jason's.

Jack was buried on the hill with his sisters. Jason remembered the ceremony well; he wasn't sad, Jack had lived a long and good life and he knew that, if only in him, Jack would live on.

Jason attended the funeral, which was held two days before his university graduation, which was attended by his proud Mum and Dad.

His father had never believed he could attain a university degree and had told Jason many times; this became Jason's creed and the awarded merit was a reflection of the determination Jason had to prove his father wrong.

"Have you had any thought about what you're going to do with yourself when you leave university?" his father asked as they stood outside on the university lawns, "We hadn't planned on your returning home you know."

"As tactful as ever," Jason thought, and then said, "I've been accepted by the Guildhall School to study drama. It is one of the best drama schools in the country."

"Acting! Only puffs go into acting!" he said venomously, "There's no money in acting! Well don't expect any handouts from us."

He could see his Mum getting frustrated and upset at his father's outburst and Jason reached down and held her hand.

"You'll be pleased to hear that I won't ask for a penny." He was going to mention the money form Jack but felt it unnecessary.

"You won't be able to afford to live without a handout," his father said.

"Then I will prove you wrong as I did about getting my degree," Jason replied.

"Then you'll live like a pauper, most of your life on the dole."

Jason smiled, "Father, I remember someone reminding you a few years ago that money and work was not everything. He has now passed, but I will prove his lesson lives on."

Then kissing his Mum on the cheek and shaking his father's hand he said his goodbyes. He could not have imagined that those were the last words he exchanged with his father and that it was the last time he saw him.

To everyone's shock his father died in his early fifties a few weeks later of a sudden and massive heart attack apparently brought on after a petty argument about a parking ticket.

Jason's Mum was inconsolable at the funeral; there must still have been some love there. For months after the funeral whenever he visited her she was cleaning and scrubbing the house from top to bottom.

She seemed to be endlessly tidying up, throwing things out, moving things around and redecorating. She reminded him of Lady Macbeth, desperate to remove the stains that just not seemed to go away.

A few months after that she sold the big house in the Midlands she had come to abhor and moved to a pretty rose-covered cottage in Oxfordshire to start a new life and be close to her son at last. She became leader of the local WI and the Parish Council and loved her retirement in a way she could not have imagined.

Jason and Francis had become engaged and visited her every other weekend. Francis was now working as a linguist in the Foreign Office and most of Jason's work revolved around London as well.

Oh, and yes, Jason became a successful actor.

Jason Hughes is not his stage name of course but you would recognise the name should it be revealed in these pages. He has appeared at most of the theatres in the land and played the lead (including Hamlet of course) in productions at the National Theatre and Royal Shakespeare Theatre.

He has also played the lead in a number of British movies and Hollywood blockbusters. He has starred in many television series but the theatre is still closest to his heart.

It is only in the theatre, he says, that nuances of the moment can be exploited. Only in the theatre can you get that instant and unbiased feedback as to the success or failure of your work.

He's also turned to writing and a play, a novel and an autobiography are all in the pipeline.

But there I go again; this is another story and once again I run before my time.

Adieu.

Epilogue

1 Corinthians 13

1 Though I speak with the tongues of men and of angels,
and have not love,
I am become as sounding brass, or a tinkling cymbal.
2 And though I have the gift of prophecy,
and understand all mysteries, and all knowledge;
and though I have all faith, so that I could move mountains,
and have not love, I am nothing.
3 And though I bestow all my goods to feed the poor,
and though I give my body to be burned,
and have not love,
it profiteth me nothing.

He remembered those summer days in the mid-70's; the flutter of the first kiss, the smell of patchouli oil, wet afghan coats and the sound of new music, exciting and progressive. They'd be called dinosaurs – Yes, Genesis, Pink Floyd, exponents of the symphonic, the key change and outstanding musicianship, lost and gone with the age of the electronic and a throw-away society.

One album stands out for him, *'Olias of Sunhillow'* by Jon Anderson, lead singer and multi-instrumentalist of Yes, with a choir-boy alto voice which soars with his lyrics above the clouds of cathedrals. It starts with the rumble of a spaceship skimming gracefully across a dying planet. The first time Jason played it the speakers vibrated as if in an earthquake and he thought they were going to burst like eardrums.

He can listen to it on CD now of course, never the same as holding the album cover, but the music still as fresh and clear and clean and inspiring as it ever was.

It takes him back to his tiny bedroom with the frost on the windows on crisp cold mornings and the sound of the horse-chestnut trees rustling in the wind on an autumn night, or the sun shining bright through the poplar trees over towards the park in the summer, and the smell of spring rain on the dry pavements and running in rivers down the windows.

Yes; the music takes him back, but most of all it takes him back to the summer when he found his first Yes album in that shop in Wales and took it home and showed it to his aunts who, like angels, looked at in wonder and smiled. They did not perhaps like or understand the music but they understood what it was to Jason and he loved them for it. They are of course long passed but he visits their graves every spring and spends time clearing the weeds, cutting the grass and trimming the flowers he planted all those years ago. Every year they bloom to blossom as ever-opening flowers, reminding him of the force and virility of life in the earth.

Sometimes Jason plays it and can he hear the chatter and laughter in the house in Aberdovey and the bubbling of the vegetable pots in the steamy kitchen, the smell of the boiled potatoes and roast beef cooking and the gentle hum of the cars driving past the bay window.

Ty Angylion - Angel House - is still there; a quaint bed and breakfast, run by an ebullient retired couple from Lancashire whose breakfasts are five-course artery-hardening banquets which a French army could march on from Brittany to Bordeaux. He had stayed there once but of course it's all changed. Somehow the rooms now seems smaller, the hall a little darker, but most of all different, the character changed beyond recognition.

The park across the street is still there and the old Roman road leads down to the secret bay surrounded by rocks and rhododendrons. Every year Jason takes his family on a pilgrimage, they think their father a little strange and humour him. Every year the sun shines and the smell of the sea clears his head for another year.

As a tradition, on Jason's last day of the holiday, as the sun sets over the estuary with Borth across the way, they light a lantern for all those that they knew and loved and send them up into the darkness in celebration of not only their lives, but also for the others in the family they have lost. Not just to remember them but also that the memory of them will light up the world, even for a few moments.

156

On those summer afternoons as he lies on the grass and takes a nap with his children playing in the sea and Francis lying next to him reading her book, he dreams of that summer and the aunts who loved unconditionally without thinking of return and who turned an introvert, shy, selfish, weak little boy into a young man with a lust for life.

And as he watches his children, twins Jack and Clarrie, laugh and play amongst the flower borders in the park and sees them sit together on the same metal bench where another much older Jack and Clarrie sat and shared their thoughts, it warms his heart like the sun's glow.

It is in those moments that one realises that life is not the seemingly endless cycle of eat, sleep and work but the gamut of emotions, how we interact, relate and *live* with people. How we give, how we take. How we accord or discord. How we harmonise and resonate and create new symphonies of life. And imperatively, how we love.

One can only hope that at the end of one's time someone will say: "I knew them well", "they were this way or that", "they were loud or quiet", "they had charisma and lit up a room", "they were kind, they were hard or they were warm", "they were war-like or peaceful", "they were beautiful and understanding".

And just like a footprint in the sand is gradually washed away by the eternal ebb and flow of the tide of time, the image of it may be remembered making its imprint perhaps deeper, and lasting longer.

We cannot predict how we shall be remembered but one can hope it is with love, fondness and warmth. As someone who was full of life and energy, who was generous in action and thought; who gave more than they took. For we know that as the sky is blue, the sea is deep and love is eternal, these memories will be formed by what we do, our actions, now.

Those we have touched, mothers, fathers, grandparents, uncles, aunts, brothers, sisters, daughters and sons may be gone, but they themselves, their love and their words could never be forgotten.

For just as the river flows into the sea and the flowers bloom by the water and the sun warms our backs, they are eternal.

Now a middle-aged man, Jason lies with them on a beautiful lush-green Welsh hill looking out across the estuary remembering and enjoying cool breezes and hot summers days.

And he loves them and misses them dearly.

By the Same Author

Biography
1994   Vangelis: The Unknown Man

Novels
1997   *going home*.
2006   *Richard of Eastwell*
2007   The Cathar Prophecy
2009   Fairytales, Poems and Prophecies
2011   ANGEL HOUSE

About the Author

Mark J.T. Griffin

(comes from lots of different places but this time around)
was born in March 1958 in Wolverhampton.

He lives in Warwickshire with his wife Ingrid,
and Sam & Lily the Labradors.

He divides his spare time between writing, creating electronic music,
and the theatre. Since the mid-eighties he has written numerous
articles and short stories.

In 1994 he wrote the biography, **Vangelis: The Unknown Man** and in
1997 the new age adventure novel ***going home***. This was following
in 2006 by the novel *Richard of Eastwell* based on his love of history and
theatre. His third novel The Cathar Prophecy. followed in 2007 and
in 2009 Fairytales, Poems and Prophecies, his first
collection of short stories and poetry was published.

ANGEL HOUSE is his fourth novel.

Website: www.markjtgriffin.com

www.ingramcontent.com/pod-product-compliance
Lightning Source LLC
Chambersburg PA
CBHW070911030726
47504CB00005B/1549